Entranced

ENTRANCED

BY JIBBER JABBER

Cover Design by Noah Ray

ISBN 13: 978-1-948921-09-1

ACKNOWLEDGEMENTS

Gwen Peterson: Thank you for your proofreading and explaining to me what a brooch is.

Jenny Dulaney: for making sure my characters were not too brusque or incompetent.

Noah Ray: for the perfectly decrepit castle.

Celeste Mitchell: for your encouraging comments and for not holding a grudge for my Vivian from the last book.

Table of Contents

Chapter 1: Line of Succession 1

Chapter 2: Killian's Birthday...6

Chapter 3: Discourtesy...12

Chapter 4: Private Dinner 18

Chapter 5: The Mute...23

Chapter 6: The Evening Stroll 29

Chapter 7: The Meeting 33

Chapter 8: Confusing Conversation 40

Chapter 9: Voices..45

Chapter 10: Sir Aidan's Request 52

Chapter 11: Invisible Chaos 58

Chapter 12: Man of Her Dreams..65

Chapter 13: Back to Reality...69

Chapter 14: Jerald's Other Name 75

Chapter 15: Daydream...80

Chapter 16: Mythical Magic..86

Chapter 17: Lara's Rain 92

Chapter 18: Aidan's Friend 100

Chapter 19: A Secret Place...107

Chapter 20: The Lost Brooch 115

Chapter 21: The Hunt 124

Chapter 22: The Stranger..130

Chapter 23: Escape from the Tower 135

Chapter 24: Fraying...142

Chapter 25: Flight 147

Chapter 26: By Her Hands..154

Chapter 27: If Bells Still Chime 161

Author's Note 166

Preview: Luna Lore...169

Chapter 1: Line of Succession

Never before in the kingdom of Callaway had there been a more exuberant assembly gathered to witness a royal disinheritance. Though emotions cannot be objectively recorded, happiness and mirth were surely the prevailing feelings in all those waiting in the throne room. There were smiles on all faces, laughter and relaxed sighs, and even a general sensation of relief. The entire royal court was present to witness a much-awaited spectacle: the disinheritance of Jerald.

Though this disinheritance had not been officially announced by King Varden, members of the royal court were certain it would occur that very day. King Varden had already assured some of his noblemen that steps would be taken to ensure that his cousin Jerald, Duke of Birkeshire, would not succeed the throne. Several of those present even heard that the peevish young duke would be banished.

However giddy as everyone was over these prospects, some of the older nobility were wary of such extreme measures. Though Jerald was known to be a nuisance and was considered to be completely incapable of ruling Callaway, he had done nothing to warrant such punishment. If the king disinherited his cousin, it would go against the ancient laws that had been put in place to safeguard families against vindictive ruling relatives. Re-writing the rules for this one particular case could set a dangerous precedent. There was also the question of who would be declared the next heir to the throne. The king had several distant relatives who could be eligible.

Duchess Kaitlin waited impatiently with the others of her class. She was anxious for King Varden to appear, but she also searched for her cousin. Once Sir Killian entered with his wife, Katie excused herself and hastened to talk to him.

"Killian! Lara! Isn't it exciting?" she exclaimed as she embraced them.

"We don't know what's going to happen. Don't get your hopes up yet," Killian warned.

"But something will happen, something good. I know it," Katie remarked. "By the way, I'm glad you're finally here. I needed to talk to you about something."

"What is it?" Killian asked.

"Well, you see, I was going over my accounts. You know that the villagers have to pay me land taxes and then I have to pay King Varden and then he does whatever he wants to do with the taxes. I don't know exactly what he does with them. Anyway, since King Varden changed his tax rates, I don't have to pay as much, so then my villagers won't have to pay as much either, but I'm having a difficult time figuring out how much I can reduce their taxes since everyone pays a different figure depending on how much land they have or how big their homes are. Would you mind coming over to my castle and helping me sort it out?"

"Kate, I know nothing about that sort of thing."

"You don't?"

"No," he laughed. "I don't have subjects to pay me. I don't even have land taxes."

"But Lara, you pay taxes, don't you?" asked Katie.

"No."

"You don't? But you have a cottage. I know you don't pay the taxes to me, so you must pay the king directly."

"King Varden's father gave me the cottage without taxes as a sign of gratitude," she explained.

"You're very lucky then."

"Ty is a marquis," Lara reminded her. "His subjects pay him. You could ask him to help you, or you could ask another noble for help."

"Oh, I didn't think about that. I don't know if that's a good idea. I don't want the others to think I'm inexperienced, and I don't talk to Ty, not anymore. We talk, but not really. We've only said 'hello' and 'how are you' and such. Besides, he wouldn't want to help me."

"It wouldn't hurt to ask."

"Couldn't you or Killian ask him for me? Please?"

"I'll see Ty today," Killian spoke. "I'll mention it to him."

"Thank you!"

"Are you sure you want Killian to fix this for you?" questioned Lara.

"He won't be fixing it for me. I just need him to ask Ty about the taxes, that's all."

"What if you have another question? Do you want to use Killian as your go-between?"

Katie paused to consider this.

"Lara, I don't mind," said Killian.

"No, it's alright," Katie assured him. "Thank you, but I think I'll deal with this myself. I'll have to talk to him eventually anyway. I might as well start now."

"Are you sure?"

Katie nodded.

The doors opened. Everyone leaned forward to look, but it was only Jerald. As he sauntered into the room, waving about his ornamental cane, those who were constrained by courtesy gave him a half-hearted bow. Jerald walked forward without looking at the spectators. His head was tilted up, and a derisive smirk was on his face. Though some noticed with pleasure that Jerald's complexion appeared more pale than usual and his haughty steps seemed less sure.

"Kate, you'd better go back to your place," Killian advised. "They're about to start – start whatever this is."

As Katie rushed back, Killian leaned over to whisper to Lara.

"Why did you talk her out of accepting my help?"

"Kate doesn't need your help," she whispered back.

"She asked for help. There's nothing wrong with asking."

"She needs to see how much she can do by herself. If she still needs you, I have no doubt that she'll ask again."

"Perhaps you're right."

"Perhaps?"

"I don't have to concede yet. It's too early to tell."

Lara gave him a half-smile. The doors opened again. As King Varden stepped in, everyone bowed to him. He strode to the front of the room and quickly gave a formal greeting before stating the purpose of this assembly.

"I thank you for coming to hear my announcement," Varden spoke. "I have the honor and privilege of formally proclaiming that in a few short weeks, I shall be married and Callaway shall have a new queen."

Chapter 2: Killian's Birthday

Lara stood motionless as she looked over the vast empty landscape. She thought she saw something appear in the distance. She leaned over the wall, placing her hand on the parapet for balance, but saw nothing out of the ordinary. She leaned back, resuming her motionless stance on the wall-walk until she heard footsteps. She took a quick glance behind her as Killian approached.

"You shouldn't be up here," she admonished.

Killian raised his eyebrow in confusion and stopped.

"Am I unwelcome?" he asked. A surprised and somewhat amused smile began to appear.

"I didn't say you are unwelcome, only that you shouldn't be up here. You're ordered to be down there with the others."

"Ah, is that all?" Killian's smile softened as he moved to stand beside her. "I'm supposed to be on guard to protect the good people of Callaway."

"Then go down and watch them."

"Well, that's why I came up here, to protect you."

"I don't need any protection at the moment. You only came

up here because you're bored."

"I came up here to see my beautiful wife. Can you fault me for that?"

He looked at her, awaiting a response. When she said nothing, he sighed and rolled his eyes. At last, Lara turned away from the landscape to look at him.

"I'm sorry, Killian. I'm glad you came up here."

"You seem more cross than glad," he gently chided.

"No, I'm merely preoccupied. Perhaps a bit worried. There is still no sign of them."

"That's nothing to fret over," Killian assured her. "We expected them to be late."

"Not this late."

Killian nodded. He glanced behind him at the castle courtyard. Knights, nobility, and common folk littered the area. Some were unceremoniously reclining on the ground, but King Varden stood resolutely on top of the steps. His mother and cousin were inside his castle, ready to join him as soon as their guests arrived. Because of the excessive lateness, Varden had excused the nobles and commoners from remaining. Nevertheless, no one moved. They waited, far too curious to catch a glimpse of their soon-to-be queen.

Killian easily spotted the red-headed Ty among the other knights. Killian would have gestured to him, but Ty was too preoccupied, exchanging glances with Katie.

"Any word on whether or not Ty and Katie's meeting was productive?" Killian inquired.

"I've been too busy to ask," Lara admitted.

"Yes, one has to dedicate an entire afternoon to talk to Kate. You can't ask her anything and expect a short and simple answer."

"That is just Kate's way," Lara defended.

"I have an idea to help pass the time – a wager."

"A wager with whom?"

"You and me. I'll wager that Kate will make some excuse to invite Ty to her castle before the week is out."

"That's ridiculous."

"So, you don't think she will? You'll take my bet?"

"No, I mean it's ridiculous that you would make a wager against me. What is the point? You can't lose or win any money. It's *our* money."

"But it could be *your* money to spend how you choose."

"I already spend money how I choose, and you already spend – "

"It's more about the principal of the matter, Lara, the moral victory."

"There is nothing moral about making a wager on a family member and a friend. It's unscrupulous."

"You're only saying that because you're afraid you'll lose."

"You're not going to get me to place some petty wager by – "

Lara abruptly stopped. A small black speck appeared in the red and yellow sky. The indistinguishable form drew nearer until it could at last be identified as a black raven. It swooped down and landed on Lara's outstretched arm. Lara whistled to it, and the raven flew to a new perch.

"They're coming now," she announced.

Killian waited until the procession was in view before signaling to King Varden. Jerald and Juliette, the queen mother, were summoned to join King Varden on the steps.

"What is that smell?" Killian asked as the carriages crept closer.

"Dirt and unwashed knights, I imagine," answered Lara.

"The journey from Ellowyn is not far. How could they have gotten this filthy? Even if they encountered difficult terrain, they should have stopped somewhere to change the horses and clean the carriages, or at least allow the knights to bathe," Killian complained. "Instead, they march in here in all their unkempt glory? I wouldn't even presume to enter my own home in such a state."

"That's because I wouldn't let you. Why are you surprised? You didn't anticipate any respect from the baron, did you?"

"One can still hope."

After the procession was inside the castle walls and at the

stairway to the castle, Baron Lucius stepped out of a carriage, grinning ear-to-ear.

"Prince Varden!" he enthusiastically bellowed, cutting off Varden's greeting. "I beg your pardon. *King* Varden, of course. Do forgive me. Old habits, you know."

"Baron Lucius, I warmly welcome you. I hope you were able to get here without much difficulty," said Varden.

"Think nothing of it, dear king. Ah, the moment you've been waiting for has arrived."

He gestured back to the carriage. A woman with blonde-grey hair, brown eyes, a gentle face, and a willowy frame stepped out.

"Oh, not this one," Lucius chuckled. "This is my wife, Baroness Isabelle, and of course, I've brought along Marguerite. Step out, Meg."

A young woman carefully withdrew from the carriage. Her black hair and blue eyes matched those of her father's. Though Marguerite was not tall and thin like her mother, her frame was far from the rotund size of the baron's. She bowed respectfully to King Varden.

"Let me just say what an honor it is to be here," Lucius gushed. "The joining of our two houses shall be historic to say the least, commemorable to hope for the best."

"Some people like to hear themselves talk far too much," Killian whispered. He scowled at the baron. "He must derive some sadistic pleasure in forcing everyone to listen to his babble."

As Lucius droned on with his speech, the once clear sky

became dark with clouds. The slight rumbling of thunder eventually forced Lucius to abruptly cut off his speech just as he was comparing Varden and his daughter's prospective union to the unmatched potential of dry chaff. King Varden instructed everyone to come inside or return to their homes. Lara began walking to the tower door. Killian followed suspiciously.

"Did you do that?" he asked, pointing to the sky.

"Your birthday is next week, and I couldn't find a suitable present. You may consider this your gift."

Killian laughed.

"Thank you, Lara. At last, you've put your powers to good use. It's fine to use magic to win wars or save lives, but you've done the noblest deed of all: you've allowed everyone to escape the baron's speech. What would I do without you?"

"What would you do without my magic, you mean," she corrected.

"No, I know what I would do," he said as he opened the door for her. "I'd simply love you all the same."

He gave Lara a quick kiss. She pushed him away and chided him for his cheekiness, but could not help but smile.

Chapter 3: Discourtesy

"What blasted weather!" Lucius complained. "Do storms always come on so suddenly?"

"From time to time," Varden answered.

The baron's and Varden's families stood together in the great hall while Varden directed the baron's belongings to be placed in the guest chambers.

"Well, I hope you control your subjects better than your weather," Lucius remarked.

"I'll thank you not to question my ability to rule, Baron Lucius."

"Please, King Varden, I hope you do not think that I intend to be rude. My concerns are –"

"Father, you must allow King Varden to introduce us to his family," Meg interjected. "The king mustn't think we lack manners." She turned to Queen Juliette. "The queen mother, I presume?"

"Yes, allow me to make introductions," said Varden. "This is Queen Juliette, my mother."

"Even mothers get wet in the rain," she spoke.

"How unfortunate that is, indeed," Meg said.

"Yes, very unfortunate, but fortune always favors the horses, of course."

Varden continued, "And this is my cousin Jerald, Duke of Birkeshire."

"Fine, fine," mumbled Lucius. "Now, if you don't mind, we would like to eat our dinner. It is already late, so you have had plenty of time to have everything prepared for us."

"The dinner is ready," answered Varden, "but perhaps everyone needs some time to freshen up."

"It sounds as though you are not prepared."

"King Varden, that is so very thoughtful of you," Meg stated. "However, we have kept everyone waiting long enough, and I must confess that we are quite famished. I do believe our appetites take precedence over our appearance, disheveled as it may be."

"No, I – I only wished for you to be comfortable."

"Thank you, Your Highness." Meg smiled.

There was a slightly uncomfortable silence for five seconds before Varden escorted the group to the dining hall. The baron made several comments about the size of the castle, which Varden ignored.

As the first course was served, Queen Juliette began humming, which drew curious stares from the guests.

"Don't worry about Aunt Juliette," Jerald assured them. "She's been that way for years. You're probably wondering if insanity is a family trait that is passed on. We're not sure, but it's quite possible."

"Perhaps my cousin is not very hungry," Varden stated.

"What are you talking about? I haven't eaten anything for hours since they were so late."

"And you won't eat anything if you don't behave," Varden warned through a forced smile.

"Oh, don't worry about it," Lucius chided. "It's hardly a secret. We all are aware of her mental state."

"I noticed your crops are looking well," Meg interjected. "We passed by some of your fields on the journey here. I particularly noticed that the – "

"Yes, of course!" exclaimed Lucius. "You are probably wondering why we are so late. It's my wife's fault, you see. She went on a fool's errand, you might say. We couldn't find her anywhere. She does that sometimes, likes to go riding. Of course, she sometimes goes by herself, the silly thing. I always try to send escorts with her. That's what she was doing this afternoon, even though I told her we had to leave for important business. She made us all so late, we had to rush to get here before the sun set. Because of her, we could only make one quick stop to freshen up."

Lucius laughed insincerely as he sent a pensive look at Baroness Isabelle.

"Mother simply lost track of time," Meg defended.

"That happens to all of us," said Varden.

"She'd lose her head if I wasn't here to remind her to put it on straight each morning," Lucius chuckled. "Anyway, as soon as we located our missing baroness, we hastened to your little kingdom as fast as we could."

"I would hardly call Callaway 'little,' Father. Even before King Varden conquered Ellowyn, Callaway was far bigger than most of our neighbors."

"Now it's even bigger since we've acquired your lands as well," Jerald chimed in.

"Everyone knows this, Jerald. There's no need to state it," Varden grunted.

"I don't know," said Queen Juliette.

"That's no surprise," Jerald murmured as Lucius chuckled.

"Jerald, get out," Varden ordered.

The duke put down his spoon and gaped.

"What?"

"Out!"

"But I'm hungry."

"Must I order the knights to throw you out, because they will gladly oblige," Varden warned.

Jerald threw his linen napkin into his soup and stood.

"I get no respect around here," he whined. "Everyone should be mindful of my station."

He shuffled out of the room, causing Lucius to laugh once again.

"It seems you have some embarrassing family members. It is fortunate for you that my daughter brings no such unfortunate traits to the marriage bed. While I have this opportunity, I would like to put to rest any concerns you may have about her ability to conceive."

"Baron, now is not the time to discuss such matters."

"It is true that I have only one child, but I assure you that infertility does not run in my family."

"Father, perhaps King Varden can hear this some other time."

"You'll do well to stay your sweet self, Meg, lest the king think he's marrying a nosy busybody. No, we could have had more children, but my wife lost our second child, a daughter. It was her own fault. She fell from her horse."

"Baron, I don't need to hear this," warned Varden.

"It was only another daughter, but after that, she couldn't have any more children. So you see, as long as Meg does as she's told and doesn't act foolishly as her mother did, you may be able to get ten, even twelve children from her."

"That's enough!" Varden shouted.

The room went silent. The women stared down at their bowls while Lucius and Varden glared at one another. Suddenly, Baroness Isabelle stood, so Varden stood politely as well. She bowed her head to the king and scurried out of the room. She did not remember to leave her linen napkin, but kept it grasped in her hands, twisting it as she retreated.

"Send dinner to the baroness' room," Varden instructed a servant as he resumed his seat.

"And you can send it to my room as well," Lucius huffed. "As your guest and future father-in-law, I would expect more deference out of you."

"As your host and your king, I should demand more respect," Varden calmly answered. "Though I know you to be incapable of that, I must insist you at least pretend to have common courtesy. Your wife may be accustomed to your ill manners; but here, you are required to give Baroness Isabelle and everyone here the courtesy that I deem appropriate. Can you manage that, Baron?"

In response, the baron threw his linen on the ground and stormed out of the dining hall. The only noise that remained after he left was the clinking of the spoons against the bowls as well as the sound of Queen Juliette slurping her soup. When the queen finished, she stood and shook her linen, draping it over the back of her chair. Varden stood and instructed the maids to escort her to her chambers, along with the remainder of her meal. Varden sat down as the next course was brought out for the two remaining diners.

Chapter 4: Private Dinner

"Is your mother well?" asked Meg.

"No, she is not, not as well as everyone else," Varden brusquely answered. "Her 'mental state' as your father so eloquently put, is not the same as others. I do not suffer from any similar condition if that is what concerns you."

"I only meant that she left dinner early. Is she not feeling well enough to eat tonight?"

"I . . . well, she does that often. Comes and goes as she pleases."

"I see."

Varden prodded the new dish with his fork, but did not yet take a bite.

"My lady – "

"I hope you will call me 'Meg.' I am so used to being called Meg that I may not answer to anything else."

"Meg," Varden began, "this . . . engagement . . . it must seem a little unusual to you."

"Not at all, Sire."

"Varden," he urged. "Please, just refer to me by my name. We are to marry, after all."

"I don't believe it is unusual, Varden."

"But are you comfortable with this?"

"Of course. It was my idea."

"The baron – your father was the one who mentioned this plan."

"And I was the one who suggested it," Meg stated. She took a sip of wine. "It only makes sense. You conquered my Uncle Morland and defeated his army. You obtained the land of Ellowyn but perhaps not the loyalty of the subjects. They may be hesitant to serve a foreign king. Our union would ease their doubts, and my family will keep or perhaps even improve our standing in society. It was spiteful of my uncle to demote my father to a baron, however troublesome my father is. I see you do not get along well with Duke Jerald, but you still allowed him his prestige."

"I don't know if that is wise of me," Varden admitted. "At least he usually does not have much effect on my ability to rule. Not usually."

Varden at last brought the fork to his mouth and ate some food.

"No, you needn't worry about me, Varden. As I said, the entire arrangement is quite practical."

"Yes, you make it sound so. Tell me, are you always so matter-of-fact?"

"I'm afraid I am."

"There is nothing wrong with that," Varden quickly stated.

"Yes, but it does make me appear rather boring, doesn't it? Father says my only passion is in numbers, but that's not entirely true."

"Numbers?"

"It's a bit strange, but I enjoy doing sums or counting or doing any sort of number problem. I know it is not very ladylike, but I cannot help myself sometimes."

"No, I don't find it strange. I enjoy it myself," Varden admitted. "The truth is, I often count steps, subconsciously in my mind. For instance, I know that there are forty-eight steps between your chair and the door."

"Sixty-one steps for me, but my strides are not as long as yours."

"Sixty-one?"

Meg smiled.

Varden smiled and leaned forward to question her further but was interrupted by a maid entering from the hall. The maid bowed and stated that Baroness Isabelle requested to see her daughter. Meg promised to not be away very long. Varden stood and assured her he would wait.

Varden stared at the door long after she had left the room, lightly tapping his fork against the plate. He shook himself out of his reverie and asked a guard if Lara was nearby. He wanted a quick word with her. Fortunately, she was still in the castle and came right away. Varden stood and cleared the room to have a private discussion.

"Your report of Baron Lucius' daughter is not as reliable as I would have hoped," he whispered.

Lara frowned.

"In what way?" she asked.

"You told me she was unattractive."

"I told you she is plain."

"That is clearly not the truth. I cannot have my judgement so adversely affected as it was once before."

"It is objectively the truth that she is plain. She is hardly a beauty. If she appeals to you on a more personal level, I could not have accounted for that."

"Fear not, Lara, I do not mean to blame you. I simply am worried my judgement could be clouded."

"I think your worries are ill-founded, but I can keep an eye on her, if you wish."

"Yes, I would appreciate that," he confessed. "I trust you will let me know if I start making foolish decisions."

Varden tapped his fingers on the table.

"Perhaps some distance would be best," he mused. "I will ask Meg if she wishes to reside in a different castle until the wedding, away from her parents, or at least away from her father.

I think her stay would be less stressful this way."

"I can look into the matter."

"She would have to stay here for the night, but perhaps tomorrow . . . ?"

Lara nodded.

"I can arrange something," she promised.

Chapter 5: The Mute

"Welcome! Welcome!" Katie chimed. "Please come in!"

She bowed and happily escorted Meg and her entourage inside. Katie's hands fidgeted with nervous excitement, and she unknowingly tugged at the handkerchief hidden in her sleeve only to shove it back out of sight. Meg nodded politely. Katie directed the servants as to where they should put the guest's belongings. King Lucius pursed his lips and trudged behind his daughter. Upon hearing that Meg would be placed in the west wing, he brushed past Meg and stood facing Katie.

"Duchess Kaitlin, this will not do," he protested. "I am sure you mean well, but of course, you are so young and inexperienced."

"I'm sorry. I don't understand," Katie spoke.

"It is customary for guests to stay in the east wing."

"But my room is in the east wing."

"My, your castle is all topsy-turvy, isn't it?" Lucius laughed. "No, no, no, my dear child. As the lady of this castle, you should be staying in the north wing. I thought you would know that even though you are quite inexperienced."

"I do know that the north wing is customary," Katie replied. "My father used to stay in the north wing, but I grew up in the east wing, and I've grown accustomed to it."

"But you shall have to move now. Guests go in the east wing."

I have to be firm. This is my castle, after all. Why did I allow Lara to talk me into this? I hate confrontation.

"Perhaps they do in Ellowyn, but here in Callaway, guests always stay in the west wing."

"That's the most absurd thing I've ever heard," he scoffed.

"Really Father, you are being quite obtuse. I'm sure you have heard more absurd things than that," Meg gently chided. "This is Duchess Kaitlin's castle, and she may situate herself wherever she pleases." She turned to Katie and stated, "The west wing will do."

Katie smiled brightly at Meg. Meg only nodded again and tilted her head to the servants, indicating that Katie needed to give them further instructions. Katie resumed her role as host and showed Meg to her chambers. The room contained a large bed, several wardrobes, two long tables surrounded by chairs, a vanity, and a changing screen. Though the room was large, the many furnishings made it appear somewhat cramped. Katie strolled to the large window and pointed to a staff leaning against the wall.

"This is for the snakes, but don't worry, we don't have many snakes in the west wing. We have quite a few in the east wing, but I'm used to them by now. I mean, I don't like them, but I'm used to them. You get to know their habits after a while and learn how to avoid them. Well, *you* won't of course, because there aren't many here."

"Absolutely ridiculous," Lucius scoffed. "Meg, you've only done this to yourself. You may stay here, but the baroness and I shall leave before any of these savage pests attack us."

Lucius left in a huff. Isabelle gave her daughter a quick embrace and left behind him. Meg turned to address Katie.

"Could I have another bed placed in here as well?"

"Uh, of course," said Katie.

"For my maid Alma," Meg explained. "I like to keep her close by. We've become like sisters."

"Oh, of course. Of course. Where is she?"

Meg gestured to one of her maids. A young woman with blonde hair and dark brown eyes shuffled forward. Her hair was pulled back from her face, permitting Katie to see the scars on her left side. The skin had several bumps and lines, particularly on her cheek, and her left eye could only partially open.

"Hello, are you Alma?" inquired Katie.

The girl curtsied politely.

"She can't speak," Meg explained. "She was born mute."

The poor girl, thought Katie.

"Well, I shall have another bed brought in. Please, make yourself comfortable here and let me know if you need anything else."

Katie's servants furnished the room the way Meg preferred,

and she was at last left alone. Meg sank down into one of the chairs. Alma strolled over and tapped her shoulder.

"No, I'm fine," Meg said.

Alma tapped her again.

"I just can't stop thinking about King Varden. He seemed very nice."

Alma sat down across from her. She smiled and pointed to her cheeks.

"Yes, I know that should make me happy, but . . . I don't know. I expected him to be rude and ill-mannered or at least boring, not kind and sincere."

The young woman sat up straight, put her hands on her hips then on her face.

"Yes, he's very attractive too."

Alma held out her hands.

"I don't know. I guess it doesn't seem as though it's much of a sacrifice to marry him as I thought it would be. I thought I would be doing something to benefit my family and both our kingdoms. I still am, but I didn't know I would feel so comfortable with him. It almost seems as though I'm rewarding myself. Perhaps my first impression of him is incorrect, and the king is putting on a pretense."

Meg was met with a shrug.

"Don't you see how wrong this is?"

Alma pointed to her own heart then pointed at Meg's.

"Stop saying that," Meg quietly reprimanded. "I don't have a good heart. I don't deserve any of this."

The girl rested her right hand over her chest and pointed at Meg with her left.

"That doesn't matter, Alma. Your forgiveness doesn't help."

Meg stood up and wandered to the window. Alma followed. She tapped Meg's arm and pantomimed playing the piano.

"Go ahead."

Alma touched her arm.

"Yes, I'll be down. You go on ahead. I'll meet you down there."

She tugged at Meg's sleeve.

"I know you're only trying to cheer me up, but it's not going to work, not right now. Give me a few minutes of brooding. I deserve that at the very least. I'll listen to you play, but allow me some misery for now."

Alma sighed and left Meg to herself. Meg stared quietly at the knights standing guard in Katie's courtyard. The sounds of the piano eventually brought Meg out of her musings. She stepped back from the window but then abruptly looked back out again. She thought she had seen something, though she didn't know what it was. The only men outside were the knights and several servants working in the gardens. She thought she had seen someone else, but he was gone now. At least, she thought he was gone. She still felt as though she was being watched. The uneasy feeling did not disappear even after she joined Alma downstairs.

Chapter 6: The Evening Stroll

Frantic knocking on Katie's bedroom door woke the young duchess late in the night. She quickly swung her feet over the bed, threw a shawl over her shoulders, and dashed to her dresser.

"One moment!" she called.

Katie yanked open the drawer too hard, and it fell out of the dresser and crashed onto the floor. She rummaged in the now misshapen drawer and plucked out the key. The knocking did not cease until Katie unlocked her door and swung it open. Katie caught Alma as she fell forward.

"Alma! What's wrong? What happened?"

The girl tugged Katie's arm, pulling her into the hall.

"What's going on?"

Alma gestured animatedly to try to explain before giving up and instead led Katie briskly down the hall. Several servants stood in their nightgowns, observing the commotion.

"Jane, what's going on?" Katie inquired.

"I don't know, My Lady."

Katie tugged her arm loose and ran past Alma to the west

wing. She knocked on the guest chamber door but then entered the room without waiting for an answer. Inside, the two beds were both empty.

"Where is Lady Meg?" Katie asked as soon as Alma caught up to her.

The girl shook her head in distress.

"You don't know? Alright then. We'll form a search party. I'm sure she was just exploring the castle and got lost. That must be it."

Alma ran down the hall, presumably to start her search. Katie ordered the servants to wake the others and gave them directions on how they should split up and look. She then ran downstairs to the main hall.

My first real guest, and I've already lost her. She probably just went exploring, or perhaps she wandered to the kitchen to sneak in a quick snack. I sometimes do that. I'm sure everything is fine. She's not lost or injured or kidnapped or . . .or murdered. Please, don't be bleeding to death in a ditch somewhere! Pull it together, Katie. I need to alert all the knights to search the grounds for her. She couldn't have walked out the gate, could she?

Just then, the main door opened and Meg strolled inside. Katie stopped running and stared.

"Duchess, I'm sorry. Have I disturbed you?" inquired Meg.

"No . . .perhaps. I – where were you? What were you doing outside in the middle of the night? And in your nightgown?"

Meg glanced down at her blue gown, touching the large

bejeweled belt around her waist. She bashfully wrapped her arms around her, attempting to cover her exposed skin.

"Tilly, please fetch a blanket for me," Katie ordered a nearby servant.

Katie handed Meg her shawl.

"Here. My nightgown isn't as revealing as yours. I mean . . . that's not what I meant."

"Thank you very much," Meg answered graciously.

"But what were you – "

Alma emitted a cry from behind Katie as she burst into the room, embracing Meg before she had a chance to speak. By the time Meg was able to unclasp herself from Alma, Tilly had arrived with a robe for Katie.

"Thank you, Tilly."

"Duchess Katie," Meg spoke, "Please forgive me. I should have told you I enjoy going for walks."

"Walks? What do you mean? At this hour?"

"Yes, I know it sounds a bit strange, but to me it is quite normal. You see, counting steps helps me sleep. I was not particularly tired tonight, so I decided to go out and count my steps." Meg raised her hand to her head and sheepishly added, "Of course, I realize now how foolish that idea was. I should have stayed inside. Please pardon me. I didn't mean to cause any alarm."

"No, no, it's alright," Katie assured her. "I'm happy you're no longer missing. Only perhaps next time, it would be best if you stayed inside or let someone know where you're going."

"Of course."

"I've never heard of counting steps as a way to fall asleep. It seems rather strange to me. Not that it *is* strange. I only mean that it seems strange to me because I've never tried it. I'm sure it is very helpful."

"Yes, it is. Now, I believe I've caused more than enough distress. I shall return to my room."

Katie assured her that she caused no serious distress. She went in search of the rest of her servants to inform them that their guest had been found. They could all return to their rooms. When Katie's back was turned, Alma gestured to Meg in a worried manner.

"Go to bed, Alma," Meg whispered. "Don't worry about it. I'm not having this discussion. I'm far too tired."

Alma tugged at Meg's arm, but she was only ignored. Meg waved off Alma's questions and wearily climbed the steps towards her chambers.

Chapter 7: The Meeting

Not very far from Katie's castle, a tall, burly man paced back and forth in a flat plain littered with dandelions and forget-me-nots. His armor clanked and squeaked with each lumbering step. His eyes darted back and forth, scanning the field for any movement. Unexpectedly, he turned around. There was a metallic hiss as he drew his sword from the sheath. There was no one there. He sighed and removed his helmet. With the sword still in hand, he scratched his head with the handle. He returned it to its sheath, placed the helmet on his head, and continued pacing.

<<snap>>

This time, the soldier knew he heard a sound. He looked to the distant tree line. A shadowy figure emerged from the forest, making no sound aside from the stray twig he had stepped on a moment before. This man wore no armor or sword, only a wrinkled brown shirt and tan brown trousers. He did not even have any shoes. A white, blood-stained cloth was wrapped around his left hand. The breeze blew his long, scraggly blonde hair in front of his face along with a few wisps of grey. He advanced towards the soldier . . . slowly.

The soldier huffed and called out, "You're late!"

The man shrugged and did not hasten his steps.

"You're late," repeated the soldier.

"Does it matter? The plan has already been prepared."

"Does it matter?! I ought to run you through for your insolence!"

The soldier hurried to him and drew his sword.

"I am sorry to be late, but you cannot kill me. You need me to succeed," said the man.

"I can handle this by myself, Dante." The soldier smirked. "I could easily find someone else. You aren't the only one with magic. You'll be cut out of the deal!"

"I'm here now, so there's no point in shouting."

"I swear one of these days, Dante, I'll bash your head against the rocks and feed your brains to the dogs."

"You do not have any dogs, so please calm down."

"I don't take any orders from you."

The soldier held the sword up to Dante's face.

"Are we attacking tomorrow?" asked Dante.

"No! If you would listen, I would tell you! This is why you were supposed to meet me tonight."

The soldier put down his sword and tried to regain his composure. Dante stood silently.

"I have received instructions from our *master*," the soldier said the word derisively. "He says not tomorrow, but the day after we will attack. You will be there to provide our cover. If fate is with us, we succeed, we get paid, and we'll both be able to get out of here."

"The time has come for this. The balance of the world will be restored."

"Whatever. Here's your first installment." The soldier shoved a small bag of coins at Dante's chest. "I'll meet you again tomorrow night at the appointed time to go over the specific plans. I'm not telling you anything now. You'll only forget and I never repeat myself. Make sure you're here tomorrow *on time*."

"My plans may cause me to be late."

"What plans? This is your only plan now!" the soldier argued.

"I have been preparing for this moment my whole life. I must continue perfecting my magic."

"Just be ready! I'll see you tomorrow."

"Yes."

"On time!"

"Perhaps on time."

"I am the captain! You have to listen to me!"

"You are not a captain," Dante nonchalantly replied. "You are a reckless mercenary who adopted a false title. I could easily kill you if I wanted to, but fate has determined we work together. I will see you tomorrow, perhaps on time."

Dante haphazardly tied the bag of coins to his worn-out belt and strolled back into the woods. The captain, still fuming, picked up a rock and hurled it at him. The stone hit Dante's back, but he kept walking. Another rock was hurled, but this time it missed. The captain picked up a third rock. Deciding against hitting his irritating ally, he chucked it as fiercely as he could in the opposite direction.

Dante weaved in and out of the forest silently, sometimes vanishing from sight. His disappearance, along with the pale tone of his skin, could perhaps trick any unsuspecting observer into thinking he was a ghost haunting the still woods. Dante continued walking until he reached a large boulder. Water flowed out from underneath the stone, and some trickled down through the cracks, forming a small river. Dane extended his hand, touching the rock and then pressing through it. Soon, his entire body disappeared into the stone.

At first, the only sound in that part of the forest was the sound of the trickling water. Then, a slight stirring from a tree was followed by a soft thud as a gangly youth jumped to the ground. The boy appeared no older than fourteen. His whole body shook, though the night was warm and there was no longer a breeze. The boy ran without stopping until he reached the open plain where the soldier paced.

"Captain! Captain!"

"Be quiet!" yelled the soldier. "Don't draw attention to yourself."

"But, Captain . . . "

The boy panted and gasped for air. He nearly pummeled into the soldier in his hurry to reach him.

"Watch it, boy!"

"I'm sorry, Sir, but – " the boy gasped again, " Captain, you were right."

"Of course, I was."

"I was able to track the wizard this time. I went back to the spot where I had lost him last night, just as you said."

"And?"

"And now I know why I lost him last time. He walked straight into a rock! I couldn't believe it if I hadn't seen it with my own two eyes! It's impossible!"

"He can do magic," the captain calmly replied. "You can do anything if you've got magic, but now we have the advantage. We know where his hideout is. Should he double-cross us, we'll find him. Never trust people with magic."

"I know, Sir."

"Don't be insolent, boy!"

"I only meant I agree with you, Sir. I don't trust wizards either."

"And he's the squirmiest of the whole lot. I know what happened when he helped King Morland. He got him and his entire army killed. He was supposed to hide them, give them cover, but he let them be exposed and die in a rockslide."

"I know. I've heard the story a hundred times," the boy complained.

The captain raised his hand to smack him.

"But – but that can't happen to us," the boy quickly added. "Dante only did that – he only betrayed them because Morland ran out of money. We've got the big money man paying us, so that means we don't need to worry, right?"

The captain grunted and lowered his hand.

"No, I don't trust him. Money or not, he could always betray us. Dante's a strange one. Maybe Morland ran out of money, or maybe he didn't. No one knows. The dead can't speak for themselves, but we won't let him betray us. Now, we know where we can find him."

The captain and the boy began making their way to their own hideout. The captain complained about how Dante kept him waiting so late at night. The boy just nodded and agreed with everything he said.

In the forest behind the large boulder, Dante showed no signs of weariness. He knelt down by the waterfall in his secret hiding place. The mist from the water hung in the air, while long, dark shadows swam in the lake below. Dante touched the dagger lying on the ground and dragged it closer to him. He sifted his fingers through the blades of grass as he pondered.

The time is coming. It took longer than I thought, but it was my fate to wait this long. It is all coming together now. It will all work for the greater good. Only their deaths will restore order to the world. Once the wicked are purged, his sacrifice will not be in vain.

Quickly, he caught hold of a long snake slithering on the ground. With his other hand, he lifted the dagger and stabbed the snake, pinning it on its back. Dante unwound the cloth on his hand, revealing a fresh wound. He squeezed some of his blood into the squirming serpent's mouth.

"Creatura sanguinis, vita est vita tua!"

He yanked out the dagger and grabbed the snake by its neck. He then plunged it head-first into the lake. The snake thrusted its body, trying in vain to escape. Dante held it under the water until the air bubbles ceased. He continued holding it below the water for another minute before pulling it out and stretching it out on the grass. He placed his worn bandage over its face and pressed down.

"Creatura sanguinis, vita est vita tua," he whispered. Dante closed his eyes.

Suddenly, the snake lurched and screeched.

Chapter 8: Confusing Conversation

"I didn't send for a witch," Meg protested.

"I know you didn't, but it's actually common protocol," Katie chirped.

Meg stared blankly at Katie, who stood patiently outside her bedroom door.

She's still wearing her nightgown. Did she just wake up? Katie wondered. *I've been up for hours. Well, I suppose I am an early riser.*

"You seem so tired."

"Of course I was tired," Meg answered, frowning. "We recently traveled, and I am sleeping in an unfamiliar environment. It takes me longer to fall asleep."

"Lara can help with that. You see, she's my very good friend, and she's also very smart, so much smarter than I am. She can give you a sleeping tonic or something like that to help you. Then, you wouldn't need to walk around and count steps."

"It shall not occur a second time," Meg argued. "I won't disappear and inconvenience everyone again."

"Oh, it's not an inconvenience. I just was afraid you had gotten lost. If you want to walk around during the day, that's perfectly fine. However, at night – "

"I told you I won't do it again," Meg tersely answered. She brushed the dark strands of hair out of her face. "Alma usually catches me, but she must not have heard me leave the room."

"Catches you?"

"Catches – catches sight of me," Meg fumbled. "It's a common saying. She usually sees me leave, so she knows where I am. If she's not awake and I feel I must go for a walk, I usually wake her or leave a note, but I already told you I'm not doing that again. I have no desire to see a witch. I am quite well."

Meg took a deep breath and continued in a calmer tone.

"Thank you for the offer, Duchess Katie, but I must respectfully decline. I hope you will excuse me while I dress. Please forgive my absence at breakfast."

"Oh, don't worry about that," Katie answered. "I'll send Alma up to help you dress."

"I can dress myself, thank you."

Katie was left standing alone in the hallway, staring at Meg's closed door. Reluctantly, Katie shuffled back down to the main hall where Lara stood waiting. Her medicine bag was leaning against one of the columns.

"Well, that's all," Katie said with a shrug.

Lara stood and waited for her to elaborate.

"She said she doesn't want anything. I'm sorry, Lara. I should have talked to her first before sending for you, but she wasn't awake yet, and I thought she would be at least a little receptive and let you prescribe something for her. She doesn't even want to talk to you."

"If she doesn't like witches, a physician could give her a sleeping tonic."

"But she seemed so nice. Why wouldn't she like you?"

"Lady Meg doesn't know me. She has no reason to trust me with her health. If it would ease your mind, you can send for a physician."

"No, a physician wouldn't be able to help like you could. Besides, she insisted that there is nothing wrong with her."

"She's probably right, Kate. It was only one night."

"That's true. Maybe, I'm just paranoid and worried about being a good hostess, but . . . " Katie leaned close to Lara and whispered, "I think there's more to it. Lady Meg implied that she often has trouble sleeping. That's why I thought a sleeping tonic from you would help."

"I can't do anything she doesn't want, Kate."

"Yes, I know, but I also think she's hiding something. She said something about Alma. She said Alma usually – "

Katie abruptly stopped. She moved her head to look past Lara. Lara turned around to see Alma standing several feet behind her. The girl was casually poking around in a potted plant.

"Alma, do you need anything?" asked Katie.

Alma jerked her head up in surprise. She smiled and then

pointed to Lara.

"Do you need Lara?"

She nodded. Holding out both hands, she wiggled her fingers. She pulled back her arms and then repeated the motion.

"I think she's asking if you do magic," said Katie.

"I don't move my hands like that. That looks ridiculous."

"Lara, you have to answer her."

"Yes, I know some magic. I'm a witch."

Alma clapped her hands together excitedly. She pointed to herself, then lifted her arm up and stood on tiptoe.

"I'm taller than you? I – I don't know what she's saying," Lara said to Katie.

"You're asking Lara to make you taller, right?"

Alma nodded.

"No, magic doesn't work that way," Lara answered.

Alma pointed to herself again. Flapping her arms, she skipped around them in a circle. Katie laughed. Lara appeared confused, glancing at Alma's antics as though she was wondering if the girl was slightly unhinged.

"I think she wants you to turn her into a bird."

Alma stopped and clapped her hands.

"If I transformed you into an animal, I wouldn't be able to

return you to your human form. You'd be stuck as a bird."

"Well, sort of," spoke Katie. "Those types of transformation spells are very powerful, Alma. Mendel, Lara's brother, was transformed once. He doesn't live here anymore but he used to be a p – an animal. Anyway, once someone is transformed into an animal, the only way to break the spell is if the sorcerer dies or if the sorcerer gives up all his magical powers. That's what happened with Mendel, the second option, I mean. The sorcerer didn't die. He gave up his magic. If he wanted to become powerful again, he would have to start at the beginning and re-learn everything." Katie turned to Lara. "Do you think he ever did? Do you think the sorcerer can practice magic again?"

"How should I know?" Lara answered. "I need to visit a patient. I can't do anything here. Inform me if Lady Meg wants my help. I can't be stuck here all day playing charades and sharing my life story."

"You're just jealous you're not as good at guessing as I am," Katie teased her.

Lara picked up her medical bag and strode out the door. She looked behind and saw Katie trying to guess what Alma was saying. Lara shook her head and hurried on with her work.

Chapter 9: Voices

Varden knew he should try to sleep. His mind was too preoccupied, counting down how many hours of rest he would have if he happened to drift off at that moment. Two or three birds were carrying on an active conversation outside his window. Why they were chirping so loudly in the dead of night, he had no idea. He attempted to ignore the ruckus, feeling too lazy to get up and shoo them away.

He would have continued lying there had he not remembered the previous night's incident of Meg's walking excursion. Lara had told him about it. When Varden asked Meg at dinner, she had been reluctant to discuss it. She did admit that counting steps helped her sleep. Perhaps the same method would work for him. It would certainly do no harm to try.

Varden quickly dressed and left his chambers. He was determined to count his steps, determined to grow weary enough to sleep. However, his resolution gradually faded as he descended the stairs and the perplexing thoughts battered his mind.

"There must be something wrong with her," he muttered to himself. "If I look hard enough, perhaps I can find it, but is that fair? Should I be looking for fault? Why can I not accept that I am already falling for her, though it seems too easy and too soon?"

He stopped at the bottom of the staircase.

"That's ridiculous. I barely know her."

"Did you say something, Your Highness?"

Varden turned to look at the knight standing in the corner.

"Is there anything to report?" Varden asked.

"No, Sire, all is well," Sir Aidan replied.

"Good. Good. Stay alert."

"Yes, Your Highness."

Varden nodded and carried on with his stroll, walking slowly down the corridor. He passed more knights standing guard. At last reaching an empty hall, he continued quietly verbalizing his thoughts, hoping the echo would not carry his voice.

"I can't do this to myself again. I always thought I was more practical than romantic. How can I be so inconsistent? The last time I thought I was falling for someone, I put everyone at Jerald's mercy. I almost died. I also looked exceedingly foolish, which was far worse."

Varden started to chuckle to himself, but then attempted to cover it with a cough. He looked around sheepishly, but there was no one around to overhear his silly musings. He ran his hand over his forehead. Perhaps he was more tired than he thought. He turned around and retraced his steps. As the staircase came into view, he saw Sir Aidan approaching with an uneasy expression.

"What's the matter?" Varden inquired, now fully alert.

"Please excuse me, Sire," Aidan whispered. "I thought I heard noises."

"What sort of noise did you hear?"

"A man's voice."

"I see." Varden relaxed his shoulders and self-consciously answered, "Pay no mind to that. I was merely thinking aloud."

"I heard a woman's voice too."

"The queen," Varden said. "She must have wandered out of her room."

"I think the noise came from in there."

Aidan pointed to the tall double-doors.

"Well? Go and see," Varden ordered.

"But . . . I think that's the throne room."

Varden furrowed his brow. He lifted his hand and motioned for Aidan to continue, but the young knight did nothing.

"So, go in there."

"But we're not allowed in there without permission."

Varden managed to stop himself from rolling his eyes.

"When you hear a suspicious noise, you are to investigate. Understand?"

"Yes, Your Highness."

"Now go investigate."

"Yes, Your Highness."

Aidan bowed and rushed to the door. He pulled at the handle.

"It's locked," Aidan said.

Varden just looked at him.

"Oh! Right. Right."

Aidan reached for the keys on his belt and rifled through them.

"Crooked one is for the prison of crooks," he mumbled. "Darkest brown is to go down. Down what? Oh, the hall. The one that's light, for the library on the right. The one that's long is where . . . king's belong. The throne room! Sorry, I found it now."

"I doubt the queen is in there if the door is locked, but you might as well check it anyway since you've gone through all this trouble."

"It's no trouble, Sire. I'm just doing my – oh, right."

Aidan quickly unlocked the door and pushed it open. He walked inside while Varden waited, glancing in the hallway for signs of his mother. Aidan tentatively stepped back into the hall, appearing more worried than before.

"Uh, Sire . . . "

He pointed into the room. Quizzically, Varden entered. He walked past Aidan and looked around to find the source of the knight's worries. He saw nothing out of the ordinary. This time, he did roll his eyes.

"Well?" he asked.

Aidan walked in behind him and pointed again.

"She's not supposed to sit there, is she?"

Varden looked at the throne. At first, he saw nothing. The room was dark, for the moon was obscured by passing clouds. As sky cleared, enough moonlight filtered in for Varden to see the outline of a woman's figure sitting on his throne. He drew near and saw it was Meg who sat there so silently, clothed in a blue nightgown. Her dark hair was uncombed and loose on her exposed shoulders. Her eyes were staring vacantly. She sat unmoving, as if she was made of stone. Varden slowly walked up the steps. She sat there eerily, making no response. Varden reached out to touch her hand, attempting to see whether the woman was real or merely a ghostly specter. Her hand felt cold as ice, yet she did not shiver.

"Meg?"

"The time is coming," she murmured. "Everything will crumble and fall."

"What will?"

Varden placed his hands on her shoulders and gently shook her.

"Meg?"

Meg gasped and jerked backwards. She would have hit her head on the back of the throne had not Varden pulled her forward in time.

"It's alright. It's alright," Varden assured her.

She looked around wildly.

"What's going on? Where is . . . ?"

She stood and rushed down the steps. Varden followed her.

"You're in my castle. Goodness knows how you got here."

She was shivering now. Varden yanked down a banner hanging on the wall and wrapped it around her shoulders.

"I . . . I just had a bad dream."

"About what?"

She hesitated.

"I don't remember."

She looked down at the banner she now wore as a shawl.

"I can't wear this," Meg said.

"Why not? It brings out the brightness of your eyes."

"It has an ancient crest on it. It's disrespectful," she argued.

"Let's see." He tilted his head and glanced at it. "It belongs to a family that has long been dead. I'm sure they won't mind your wearing it. It looks much better on you than on the wall anyway."

Meg smiled at Varden, a relaxed smile that smoothed out the worried lines on her forehead and created crinkles around her eyes.

"What do you want me to do, Your Highness?" Aidan asked.

Varden turned around. He had completely forgotten about him.

"Send one of the queen's servants to check her chambers. We'll ensure my mother is still there. Then, we will escort Lady Meg back to Duchess Kaitlin's castle."

"I'm so sorry," said Meg. "I got distracted by counting steps. I won't wander off again."

Varden gently led her out of the room.

"I wish I could believe that," he stated, "but I'm afraid I don't."

Chapter 10: Sir Aidan's Request

Before Lara arrived at Katie's home, Lady Meg had already departed despite the early hour. She had commissioned some knights to escort her to King Varden's castle. Katie tried in vain to convince her to stay, for how would Lara be able to help if Meg wasn't there? But Meg would not stay or even return so long as "that witch" was near. Meg would see a physician at King Varden's castle, and that would have to do. She assured Katie she would return for dinner once Katie's castle was rid of any old crones. She then briskly left before Katie could protest further.

Katie tried to enjoy her breakfast of barley and figs, but she felt rather alone in her large dining hall. She never before noticed how much she disliked this room. The table was far too long. The doors, too tall. A large banner covered one part of the wall, but she could still see the bright stones that contrasted with the older, dustier ones. Some time ago, a dragon had burst through that wall, making it necessary to replace that section with new stones, but no attempt to get the old section of wall to match with the new had ever proved successful. She would have to replace the whole wall.

She tossed down her spoon, which clanked on the table, the noise echoing throughout the large, bare room. What did she care about stones?

I'm such a terrible host, a terrible duchess. I don't know anything. Twice now, I've misplaced my guest, and I can't seem to make her happy. Is there nothing I can do?

"Kate?" Lara called as she opened the large door. "I knocked twice."

Katie bolted out of her seat and nearly knocked Lara over in her embrace. She wanted to tell Lara how stressed she was, but she stopped herself. That would be selfish, for Lara had to focus on helping Meg with . . . whatever was wrong with her. Katie explained to Lara as tactfully as she could the reason Meg was not on the premises.

"Then I'll have to do what I can here," said Lara. "I'll take a look in her room. Maybe I can find out what's causing her to sleepwalk."

"You think it's magic?!"

"No. No, I didn't say that."

"But you think it is, don't you?"

"Kate, anyone can have bad dreams and sleepwalk. I'm sure it's a natural, unmagical occurrence, but I'll see if something she is taking is making it worse."

"Like magic!"

"No, don't say that. That doesn't mean it's magic. Don't tell Lady Meg you think it's magic. Your speculations will only worry her."

"I know. I know. If she's wary of witches, she'll be terrified of magic. I won't say anything unless we know for sure, but I think it is magic. That reminds me of something I wanted to tell you! I've been practicing an awful lot, and I think I can finally - Oh! I know! You should talk to Alma! She's still here. She didn't leave with Meg."

Lara grimaced.

"I'm not good with children," she admitted.

"Oh Lara! Alma's not a child. She's probably only a little younger than I am."

"She acts like a child."

"No, she doesn't. She just has to act everything out. That's how she communicates."

"I'd understand her better if she would write it down."

"For goodness sake, Lara, I'll talk to her then."

"No, I'll do it."

"Alright, good. She's in the garden. Do you want me to come with you? I can probably help. I understand her very well."

"You may want to stay here."

"Why?"

"I thought I saw Sir Ty coming this way."

Katie crossed her arms in front of her and said, "How strange. I don't recall inviting him. No matter. I'll see what he wants."

Lara nodded then turned and left the room. As she walked

outside into the brisk air, she nearly collided with Sir Ty.

"Sorry, Lara," he apologized.

"Watch your step," Lara quietly cautioned.

She wandered into the garden to find Alma. A servant led Ty inside the castle to Katie, who begrudgingly granted him entrance.

"Why are you here, Ty?" she asked once they were alone.

"It's only a matter of business," he attempted to assure her. Katie resumed her seat, but Ty stood uncomfortably near the other end of the table.

"I appreciate your help with the matter of the taxes."

"You're welcome, but this is something else. Do you know Sir Aidan?"

"No."

"He's a good knight. He's actually from Ellowyn, but he's proved his loyalty to Callaway. He's young, probably too young to even be a knight, but he's very bright and brave and loyal. Anyway, he is currently serving at King Varden's castle, but Aidan asked me if he could be sent here for a while. I know it's quite unusual – "

"But you decided he could be stationed here? Without consulting me?" Katie demanded.

"Cripes, Katie. What do you think I'm doing right now?"

Katie's chair dragged against the floor as she stood up.

"But you've already told Sir Aidan you would arrange it."

"I've done nothing of the sort," Ty argued.

"You always do this, Ty. You think that since I asked for your help in one matter that you can control my life in every other way."

"I'm not doing that!" Ty clenched his hand and raised it as though he would thump it against the table, but soon thought better of it. "I only told him I would ask. I made no guarantees," he said in a calmer tone.

Katie looked at him suspiciously.

"I know how controlling I was in the past. I'm not making that mistake this time, Katie."

Katie folded her arms and turned her body slightly away from him.

"Why does Sir Aidan want to be sent here? It sounds as though he has an enviable position at the king's castle."

"Aidan says he wants a temporary change of scenery, though I suspect it is not the scenery he wishes to see."

Katie could not help but smirk.

"What? You think he fancies someone here? Who?"

Ty smiled as he answered, "I have no idea. The poor kid blushed at the mere mention of the idea and refused to tell me anything more."

Katie laughed softly and shook her head. She thought for a

moment before answering.

"If he causes any trouble, including any unwanted attentions, he's out."

"Thanks, Katie. I shall inform him immediately."

Both of their smiles faded as silence permeated the room.

"I miss you, Katie," Ty admitted.

"You still see me every now and again."

"I know. I still miss you."

"I thought you were going to inform Sir Aidan immediately."

Ty nodded.

"Goodbye," he spoke.

Ty bowed and strode to the door. Katie took several steps forward, following him, before calling out.

"Ty!"

He stopped and turned around.

"I miss you too."

Ty smiled widely.

"I'm glad to hear it."

"I think – "

Katie's words were cut off by the yells of her knights.

"Attack! We're under attack!"

Chapter 11: Invisible Chaos

"Stay here," Ty ordered Katie as he charged out of the room.

"Not on your life," she shouted back. "I will defend my home."

As they ran past the windows in the hallway, Katie could see the arrows whizzing by outside. She pushed a window open and began to lean out. When Ty saw her, he shouted and quickly ran over to her, pulling her back inside.

"Don't do that! You can't go out without armor!"

"I just wanted to look," Katie explained. "I can't tell what's going on!"

"I swear you'll be the death of me, Katie."

"Sorry."

Ty hurried to go outside and join the fight. Katie stopped a knight who was rushing past.

"What's going on?" Katie demanded.

"People are shooting at us, My Lady," the knight answered.

"Who is? How many are there?"

"I don't know."

"Well, get back out there then!"

"Yes, My Lady."

Katie bolted to the steps. She needed to get a higher, safer view, to determine the course of action. The servants were frantically running down as Katie dashed up the stairs. She ordered all of the servants to the cellar as she ran. Once she reached the top, she headed towards the nearest tower.

She abruptly halted. Katie felt a . . . presence. No, it was more than that. She thought she felt a slight breeze, a breeze that did not arise from a morning wind. It was the slight wisp of air one feels as someone else hurries past. Katie felt there was something heavy in the air. She was drawn to the west wing. She softly stepped into the west hallway and stopped. All of the doors had been flung open.

She tried to shake off her uneasy feeling. It all meant nothing. Nothing was out of the ordinary here. The servants knew well to keep the doors closed, but perhaps their minds were too preoccupied in their haste to leave. That must be it.

Katie felt a cold hand grab her arm. She jumped and let out a yell, which was quickly followed by a sigh of relief when she saw it was only Alma.

"I'm sorry. You scared me. Quickly, you must go to the cellar. We're under attack."

Alma shook her head. She wiggled her fingers in front of her.

"A witch? Lara?"

The girl pulled her arm back as though she was pulling on a bow string.

"Lara is shooting arrows?"

Alma punched herself in the stomach.

"She's been shot? Where is she? Show me!"

Alma and Katie ran down the stairs. Katie heard Ty's voice echoing in the hall. He was arguing with someone. Katie recognized Lara's voice yelling back and felt immense relief.

" . . . with respect, or at least treated with some decency!" Lara was shouting.

"I did not manhandle you!" Ty yelled back.

"You dragged me in here!"

"I pulled you to safety, Lara! You've been shot!"

"You pulled me away from helping!"

Lara sat in a chair near the dining hall door. She was trying to press a cloth into her side to slow the bleeding, all while arguing with Sir Ty, who stood by with an exasperated look on his face.

"Lara!" Katie called.

"I'm fine, but don't ask me what's going on, because I was dragged away before I could be of any use to anyone," Lara complained.

Katie glanced out the window. She heard the commotion of her knights rushing by, but there were no longer any arrows being shot.

"What happened? Has the attack stopped?"

"What?" Lara asked. "Did they run away? We need to track them down."

"Lara, please stay here," Katie requested. "Killian will be so put out with me if you leave before you're treated."

"As long as we're quick about it," Lara conceded. "Just make sure *he* doesn't manhandle me again," she said, glaring at Ty.

"I didn't manhandle y– fine. I won't," Ty said.

He quickly ran outside before Lara could argue with him further.

"I might have been too harsh with him," Lara admitted after he left.

"Worry about that later. Alma and I can move you to the library," Katie suggested. "We'll be able to help in privacy. Where did you leave your bag?"

"I left it by the front door. Don't move me to the library. I'll bleed all over the rugs."

"We'll at least get you into the dining hall. Alma, please fetch . . . "

Alma had already returned with Lara's bag in hand. They helped Lara walk through the doors and to a chair. Katie ordered a knight to stand outside and ensure they would not be disturbed. Katie rifled through Lara's bag for the necessary supplies and began working. Alma remained near, walking anxiously around in circles.

"You'll need to wrap it tighter," Lara instructed.

"I know. Are you sure you're going to be alright?" Katie asked.

"I'll be fine."

"Are there many casualties?"

"I don't know. Your knights are probably tending to any wounded if they are not tasked with tracking whoever attacked."

"We can help them after we take care of this. Do you know who was attacking us?"

"No, I didn't see them. I don't think anyone saw them."

"They were wearing masks?"

"I saw no one. Nothing. No mask, no people. I don't know where the arrows were coming from. It was as though they appeared out of nowhere. I was shot first and was too preoccupied to investigate further. Did you see anyone?" she asked Alma.

Alma shook her head.

"It was over too quickly," Lara stated. "Perhaps they shot once and then immediately ran off."

"How very strange."

"Yes, it is strange." Lara looked down. "I don't mean to be rude, but are you almost done?"

Not very far away, Dante rode on horseback, leading twenty soldiers behind him. The soldiers wore ill-fitting armor melded together with diverse metals and different coat of arms. In the rear, a gangly boy wore no armor as he rode a speckled mare. The captain rode directly behind Dante, looking none too pleased. Dante slowed his horse once they reached the woods. He turned to speak to the captain.

"I will cover your tracks," Dante spoke. "They won't be able to follow you."

"Dante! I've had enough of this! Why did you order the retreat!" shouted the captain.

"Because she wasn't there."

"She was!"

"I checked myself. She was not there."

"She must have been hiding!" the captain argued.

"No, I told you this morning she was not there. You should have listened to me."

The captain spurred his horse closer to Dante's.

"I do not take orders from you," he spoke with menace. "My source told me she was there!"

Dante calmly answered, "My source told me she was not."

"What source? You don't have a source."

"Why do you think I was late this morning?"

"I know she is staying there!"

"Yes, she is staying there, but she was not there this morning.

We can return another time, but we cannot take her now. Go, and I will cover your tracks."

"You'd better be right about this, Dante! Come on, troops!"

The captain, his men, and the boy rode into the woods. When the sound of pounding hooves began to fade behind him, Dante breathed in a slow, deep breath. At last, he was alone. With eyes closed, he let out the breath and relaxed his shoulders, enjoying the serenity and quiet.

The time is coming.

Chapter 12: Man of Her Dreams

Meg closed her eyes. Perhaps if she tried again, she would wake up and be back in bed. She blinked several times. No, she was still there, stuck in her dream. She knew she must be dreaming, for she saw a blue and purple spotted squirrel run in front of her and disappear. Meg knew she should be at Katie's castle. Was she still in her room, or was she sleepwalking again? She couldn't remember walking past Alma. She couldn't have walked past the extra guards outside her room. Why were they stationed there? For added security? Yes, she remembered now. Bandits had attacked the castle earlier. They even shot the witch. Meg wondered if the old crone was alright.

She stumbled slightly. She glanced down at her feet. At least she was wearing her slippers this time. She watched the blue slippers drag against the grass. She knew she was outside and that it was dark. She was walking up a hill. If she was awake now, she should go back to the duchess's castle. Meg tried to turn around but she could not stop walking forward. She felt herself being pushed along. Someone was holding onto her.

Meg slowly turned her head. A hooded figure was beside her, forcing her onward.

"No!" she shouted. "Not him again!"

She tried to break free. The hooded man held onto her and pressed a handkerchief over her face. Meg hated that smell. She closed her eyes.

When she could see again, she was surrounded by birds. Their feathers were black, but they were not ravens or crows. She observed with dismay as their faces changed and morphed into the faces of humans. Meg kept walking and tried not to look at them. They flew around her for what seemed like hours until at last they disappeared. Then Meg smelled the strange scent again.

She blinked. She was somewhere else now. She watched a dog and a horse float past her. She could faintly hear her own footsteps treading on the ground. It was not a scraping sound one hears when walking on a dirt path. It was not the soft tread as one walks on grass. Meg tried to see, but her eyes would not focus. She walked past a knight. He seemed real, but he did not acknowledge her presence. She managed to slip off her left slipper. She could feel the cold, smooth stone. Then, she felt a carpet. Her eyes began to see more. She was inside a castle.

"Am I back?" she wondered aloud.

A hand quickly covered her mouth. She tried to fight, but it was of no use. At least it was not the awful smell. She tried to relax. If she resisted, the dream would only be prolonged.

The hooded figure beside her led her down a hall. He opened a familiar door, and they both walked through. Meg knew where she was now: inside King Varden's throne room. The man quietly shut the door behind them. He released Meg and moved to stand in front of her. As he removed his hood, revealing his scraggly blonde hair, Meg looked away. She didn't want to see his face.

"I told you the time was coming," he whispered. "The time when injustice shall be punished. The high and mighty who wield absolute power will be brought low. Everything happens for a reason, and everything in the past has led to this special purpose. Terrence – "

"Don't say that name," Meg begged.

She covered her ears, but still she heard the man's voice.

"His death had a purpose," he went on. "It spurred my hatred of your kind. Had Terrence not died, I would never have realized I was the most powerful wizard in the universe."

"Please leave me alone."

He shook his head.

"I cannot do as you ask. You are the cause of this. You will see everything to the end. You will see the revolution. See the corrupt rulers beg for mercy that will not be granted. Everything around you will crumble and fall so that mankind can start anew. I told you the time was coming."

"Stop saying that," Meg whispered.

Dante smiled. He lifted his arms.

"The time is now."

He clenched his hands into fists and pressed them against the ground. Suddenly, the castle began to shake. Meg looked up. The ceiling above her was starting to crack. She turned around and pulled on the door, but it was locked. Meg sprinted across the room just as the ceiling collapsed. She ran to a wall, but it began to rock back and forth, then lean towards her. She tried to quickly dodge out of the way, but she twisted her foot and fell. She raised her hands over her face as the wall crashed on top of her.

Chapter 13: Back to Reality

Varden paced back and forth across Meg's room as he rubbed the back of his neck. He stretched his hands out in front of him, then clasped them behind his back before he returned to massaging his neck. He briefly ceased pacing to voice his thoughts.

"I just don't understand how with all these guards – "

He stopped talking when he saw that Lara would not hear, for she had fallen asleep in her chair. Varden resumed his agitated movements until at last he saw Meg begin to stir in her bed. He tapped Lara's arm.

"Lara! She's waking up."

Meg opened her eyes. She saw she was back in Katie's castle and sat up in bed.

"Meg," Varden spoke, "I'm sorry. I know it is not the usual protocol for me to be in your chambers."

Meg raised a hand to her neck but then realized she was already modestly covered in a robe. Did she fall asleep wearing this?

"Where is Alma?"

"She is eating breakfast. She wanted to remain by your side, but I insisted she should eat something. This is Lara." Varden gestured to the woman in the chair.

"The witch?" asked Meg. She stiffened. "I thought witches were older."

"No," Lara answered.

"I'm sorry, but I do not want to see any witches."

"Please give Lara a chance," Varden spoke. "She has been invaluable to me, and I believe she can help you."

"Help? There is nothing the matter with me."

"What about your sleepwalking?" Varden asked.

Meg gasped. "The castle!"

She bolted out of bed but immediately stumbled. Varden swiftly moved forward and caught her.

"My foot," Meg explained. "I twisted it last night."

"I looked at your foot. It doesn't seem to be badly hurt," Lara spoke. "Nothing is broken. It appears to be only bruised, not twisted."

"No, I twisted it. It was last night when the castle fell."

"The castle didn't fall," said Lara.

"Not this one, obviously. King Varden's."

"My castle?" asked Varden.

"Yes! Isn't that where you found me? Why else are you here?"

Lara got up and strode across the room to the window.

"The last thing I remember," Meg continued, "I was in your throne room being buried by all the rubble and – "

Lara pulled back the drapes and stepped aside. Meg stared incredulously at Varden's castle. It was still standing intact. Meg scanned the room for her blue slippers. They were both beside her wardrobe. She groaned and sat down on the edge of her bed. Varden kept his hand on her shoulders.

"Of course. It was a dream."

Lara pulled a chair to the side of the bed and sat.

"I would like you to tell me about your dream," Lara said.

"Why do you need me to tell you?" Meg asked in disbelief. "Don't you already know? I thought witches had the power to read minds."

"No, we can't read minds. Is that why you didn't want to see me? Were you afraid I would read your mind?"

"Why do I need to discuss my dream? I'd rather not think about it."

"I need to know how much of it was real," Lara insisted.

"None of it was real. It was a dream."

"You hurt your foot. Was that in your dream?"

"Yes," Meg confessed, "but I must have done that in my

sleep. I must have hit it against a banister or the wall. I've been in this room all night."

"No, you haven't. King Varden found you unconscious in his throne room."

Meg shook her head and looked around the room.

"No, how could I have left?"

Lara shifted forward in her chair.

"Why do you keep looking at your slippers?" Lara asked. "Is it because you lost one last night?"

Meg stared at her.

"When King Varden found you, you had only one slipper. The other was found in the corridor."

"I was found in the throne room?"

She looked up at Varden who nodded.

"I don't know how you got in. The door was locked," Varden remarked.

Meg raised her hand to her head and rubbed it in confusion.

"Last night, did you feel the ground shake?" Lara continued questioning.

"Yes!" Meg exclaimed. "Everything was shaking and the castle walls crumbled. How did you know that?"

"The castle is still there, as you can see," Lara stated, "but there was a sort-of earthquake last night."

"A sort-of earthquake?"

"Only King Varden's castle and the nearby grounds felt the earth shaking. No one here at Katie's castle felt it. I certainly didn't feel it."

"What does that mean?"

"The ground did shake, but it may not have been naturally caused. Normally, earthquakes are felt by many others, not just people in one small area. This earthquake may have been the product of magic."

Lara stood and went to Meg's vanity. She picked up a bottle of oil and handed it to her.

"I have been examining your things since yesterday."

"I don't recall giving you permission to examine my things."

"Do you use this oil every night?" asked Lara, ignoring Meg's irritated comment.

"Of course," Meg answered. "A merchant sells these back in my kingdom."

"It contains nightshade."

"So?" Meg shrugged.

"Lara says nightshade can cause hallucinations," Varden explained.

"I don't know if it can cause someone to sleepwalk," Lara continued. "How long have you used this oil?"

"I've been buying it for years."

"How long have you been sleepwalking?"

"Long before that. Ever since I – I was little. No, not little. I mean, younger. Over the past few months, I have been sleepwalking more frequently. I also have nightmares now. I hardly ever had dreams before."

"They may not be dreams," said Varden. "They could be hallucinations. Some of it could even be real."

"Which is why you must describe your dreams to us."

Varden glanced at Lara, not wanting her to push Meg too much. Meg reluctantly obliged. She began by explaining that the hooded man with blonde hair was a constant haunt in her sleep.

"Is his name Terrence?" asked Varden.

"What?" Meg gasped. "Where did you hear that name?"

"From you. You were mumbling that name when I found you last night."

"You didn't mention I was mumbling things," Meg stammered. "No, that's not his name. I don't know who he is. This man keeps repeating that name to me. He also constantly says that the time is coming and that he will bring down the powerful. I'm not sure what he means though. It's all nonsense."

Lara tilted her head and narrowed her eyes. She studied Meg closely as she continued describing her dreams.

Chapter 14: Jerald's Other Name

Alma wandered up the stairs, rubbing her tired eyes. She went to Meg's room, but an old knight was standing guard, ensuring that no one interrupted the meeting between Varden, Meg, and Lara. Alma tried to persuade him to let her pass, but the knight refused. She sighed and went to the next room over. She opened the door and saw Jerald, Duke of Birkeshire, hunched over with his ear pressed into the wall, endeavoring to hear whatever secret business his cousin was conducting. Alma hurried over and tugged his arm.

"Get off – "Jerald began to scold, but he quickly lowered his voice to a whisper. "Get off me you ugly wretch."

Alma stepped back as he swung his cane at her.

"Don't you know who I am?"

She shook her head.

"I am King Varden. I am the ruler of this kingdom, so I can listen if I please."

He put his ear back to the wall. Alma appeared perplexed, unsure whether or not to believe him. She was sure the king was in the room with Meg. She tugged Jerald's arm and pulled him away from the wall once again.

"Don't touch me you scarred mutant," he whispered angrily. You will show me some respect. Bow to me, peasant. Bow to your king."

He whacked Alma with his cane.

"I said bow to me. Get on your knees."

He struck her again. The distressed girl did as she was ordered.

"Are you going to accost me again? Hmm? Don't look up at me. Keep your head down. Are you going to accost me again?"

She shook her head. Jerald raised his chin and looked even more cocky.

"Beg for mercy then."

When she said nothing, Jerald hit his cane against the floor with a <<thwack>>. He was so engrossed in his small claim of power, he did not notice the approaching footsteps.

"Go on, beg," Jerald ordered. "Your king demands it."

"What is going on here?" Sir Aidan asked as he stepped into the room.

He stared incredulously at Jerald, disgusted but also marveling at his utter foolishness.

"Stay out of this, peasant. Know your place."

"My place is to serve the king. The actual king. This is now the second time this week, to my knowledge, that you have impersonated King Varden just to torment someone who did not recognize you," Aidan scoffed.

"You still have to obey me. I am the Duke of Birkeshire," Jerald protested.

"And you, Duke, have intruded into Duchess Kaitlin's castle." Aidan grabbed Jerald's arm. "I shall see you are put out."

The young knight dragged him out of the room despite Jerald's protests. Aidan pulled him down the hall and to the stairs, where they encountered Ty and Katie.

"Jerald!" Katie exclaimed. "What are you doing here? Get out!"

"Thank you, Sir Aidan," Ty spoke as he grabbed Jerald's other arm. "I shall see to it the duke is thrown out – excuse me, escorted out, with Duchess Kaitlin's permission."

"Granted," said Katie.

"Unhand me!" Jerald yelled. "I can see myself out!"

Nevertheless, Ty did not release him. Now free of his task, Aidan returned to the room where he had found Jerald. Alma still knelt on the ground with her head bent.

"It's fine to get up now," said Aidan.

Alma's shoulders shook slightly.

"Oh."

Aidan knelt down beside her and handed her a handkerchief.

"Here. You can have this. It's clean. I promise."

Alma took it and held it to her eyes.

"I actually used to be afraid of Jerald. I thought he was powerful because he's the king's cousin, but he's actually rather sad and pathetic. I think he's only pretending to be King Varden because he can't use his own name anymore. He's constantly mocked. No one respects him. I doubt there's a bigger fool than Duke Jerald."

Alma sniffed and pointed at herself.

"No. No, you're not a fool at all. You didn't do anything wrong. Jerald – he just took advantage of the fact that you're new. I know what it's like to be new in a different land. Everything and everyone is strange and even scary."

Alma handed him back his handkerchief. Aidan took it and handed her a different one.

"Here, you can keep this one just in case you need it later. I always carry two."

Alma accepted it and set it on her lap.

"Do . . . do you still play piano?"

Alma looked at him quizzically.

"Well, you see, I'm actually from Ellowyn, and I used to clean the chimneys and fireplaces, and there was this nice girl at Baron Lucius's castle, and she used to play the piano and be nice to me, and we'd just spend time together. She – she probably wouldn't recognize me without all the dirt and the soot. Probably wouldn't remember anyway."

He glanced at Alma. She smiled then looked away.

"Do you think maybe I'll get to hear you play again?"

The blushing girl tried unsuccessfully to hide her smile as she nodded.

Chapter 15: Daydream

After the noon meal, Meg declared she would go upstairs to rest. Katie expressed her concern, having already lost her guest three times. Meg assured her she would be fine now that Lara had taken away her nightshade-infested oil.

"I have never been known to sleepwalk in the afternoon," stated Meg.

"Will Alma go upstairs with you?"

"No, she wanted to play on your piano. I believe I already hear her playing now."

"I can send her upstairs, or I could go upstairs myself."

"No, please, I will be fine. I'm sorry I have caused you so much distress, Katie." Meg smiled and put her hands on Katie's shoulders. "You truly are a wonderful host. I doubt anyone else could have managed all my troubles as well as you."

"Thank you." Katie breathed a sigh of relief. "That means a lot to me. Wait. At least let me have someone stationed outside your door."

"If I will make you feel better."

"It would. Oh, I forgot to tell you: Lara will be back here

soon. I think she wants to talk to you again."

"That's fine. Let me know when she is here, and I shall see her."

Meg took a step, but then turned back.

"Katie?"

"Yes?"

"Were my parents told I was found in Varden's castle this morning? Do they know about the incidents of last night?"

"Um, I'm sure King Varden told them you had been sleepwalking again. He may have left out some details, but I'm sure they know what happened."

"While I slept this morning, did they come to see me?"

"Well, no, but I'm sure King Varden told them that you were alright and that he . . . he probably assured them that he could take care of the . . . situation."

Meg nodded her head and gave Katie a smile that did not quite match the look of sadness in her eyes. She thanked Katie, left the dining hall, and went upstairs. Once a knight was stationed outside her room, Meg closed and locked her door, putting the key on top of one of the tables. Counting her steps, she wandered to her bed. She closed her eyes and sat down. Meg wasn't actually tired. She just needed someplace quiet to think. Someplace private where she could throw away the dark memories without others watching her and thinking her to be somewhat insane.

She heard a creak on the floor behind her. Perhaps she was

insane. Right now, she hoped she was. Please let that sound be the conjuring of an overactive imagination. It was an unusual wish, and one that would not be granted. She stood up and turned around slowly, filled with dread.

The hooded man stood there, though he was no longer concealed in a cloak. Instead, he wore a wrinkled brown shirt and brown trousers. He smelled musty, the smell of unwashed dirt and sweat. His left hand was wrapped in a cloth that was stained red.

"Maybe I fell asleep," Meg whispered to herself.

The man took a step towards her. Meg ran to the door, forgetting she had locked it. She twisted the handle in panic.

"Don't scream," Dante whispered. "We must talk."

Meg stood, frozen with fear. The knight outside knocked on the door and asked if all was well. Meg made no sound. She couldn't take her eyes off the intruder. The knight again asked if she was alright. Dante took hold of the door handle and opened the door just slightly, hiding behind it.

"Is everything alright?" the knight asked.

Meg stared at him, not knowing what to do or how to answer. Petrified, she nodded her head.

"I thought I heard something," the knight queried.

"No," Meg croaked. She cleared her throat. "All is well. Go and tell Duchess Kaitlin I don't want to be disturbed. I'm applying my *night oil* and plan to sleep for several hours. I don't want anyone stationed outside."

"Yes, My Lady."

The knight left to deliver the message. Dante shut the door.

"I am glad you came upstairs," he said. "I need to talk to you. It would have been difficult if you hadn't come up here alone. Fate is a marvelous thing, is it not?"

"What is it you have to say?" Meg asked in a shaky voice.

"There are men coming soon. They plan on taking you. They think I am working with them. They call me 'Dante,' but that is not my name. Only you know my name."

"No, I do not."

Dante slowly reached out and put his hands on her shoulders. Meg shuddered.

"Marguerite, you must not fight fate. Everything happens for a reason."

"Why must you say the same thing over and over again?"

"I will say it until you believe it."

"I don't believe anything you say. You are clearly old and have become senile."

"I neither look old nor sound senile." He took hold of her hands and led her to the window. "The thugs who are working for me have their plans, but they will fail, for they do not understand that destiny has brought us down this path."

Dante smiled and exhaled deeply.

"It is not yet time for you to be taken."

"And when will that time be?" inquired Meg.

"It will happen once I have accumulated enough creatures."

Meg hesitated to ask.

"What creatures?"

His smile widened.

"I knew you would want to see," he said with pride.

There was frantic knocking at Meg's door, along with the jostling of the door handle.

"Meg! Open the door!" Katie's voice called.

Meg didn't move. Dante reached behind the large velvet drapes and revealed a ginormous burlap sack. It seemed heavy as he hefted it up. It was filled with something that squirmed.

"They used to be normal, but they have been transformed with blood magic. Killed and given new life, new purpose."

"Just break it down!" Katie ordered someone.

Dante was practically beaming as he stared fondly at the bag.

"I call them Nahiri," he said.

Meg recoiled in horror and slumped against the wall. She heard the knights ramming against the door as she sank to the floor.

"No! This isn't real! It's a dream! It's all a dream!"

"Meg! Meg!"

Meg looked up. The knights had broken through the door, and Katie was rushing over to her. She knelt down beside her. Dante was nowhere in sight.

"He was here," Meg whispered.

"Search the grounds," Katie ordered her men. "Someone broke into this room. Be careful. The intruder may have magic."

Katie led Meg to a chair and offered her a glass of wine. A servant brought a bottle and glasses, which Meg gratefully accepted. No one noticed the burlap sack on the floor that protruded from behind the velvet drapes.

Chapter 16: Mythical Magic

"Lara! The man was here! Meg said his name is Dante!" Katie shouted. "Wasn't that the wizard who was rumored to have helped King Morland?"

Lara set her bag down on the floor near Meg's broken-down door. Before she could answer, Meg stood up and added, "He said he's using blood magic!"

"And he's making a lot of them!" said Katie.

"A lot of what?" asked Lara.

"And there's going to be an attack soon!"

"And Meg's going to get kidnapped later!"

"But he wouldn't say when!"

Lara calmly walked over to Meg and Katie. As she stepped, she leaned slightly to her left and briefly touched that side which had been struck by an arrow yesterday. Katie noticed this slight motion. She frowned with worry. She wanted to say something, but knew Lara would not appreciate attention being drawn to it.

"You're going to have to start your explanations again, but slower this time," Lara stated.

"There isn't time!" Meg exclaimed. "He's using blood magic!"

"What is blood magic?" asked Katie.

"There's no such thing," said Lara.

"You must know something about it," Meg insisted.

"I know it doesn't exist."

"At least tell us what you've heard," Katie prodded. "Tell us any stories you may have encountered. Whether it's true or not, this man Dante clearly believes it, and we should understand what he believes so we know what he's planning."

Lara relented, "I only know that people would sometimes tell stories of this type of magic. That somehow wizards or witches would use their own blood to make strong and powerful creatures who are loyal only to them."

The sack behind the drapes moved slightly.

"Is it similar to a transformation spell then?" asked Katie.

"I suppose in theory."

Katie surmised, "Then the only way to get rid of the powerful creatures would be to either convince the wizard to give up his magic – "

"Which he would never do," Meg interjected. "He's too insane."

" . . . or kill the wizard. Then the creatures would return to their normal state, whatever state that is."

"Except this type of magic isn't real," Lara insisted. "I have seen many things and traveled many places. Never have I ever encountered anything resembling this fabled magic."

"Dante has used it," Meg declared. "He was even going to show me. I didn't see it because it was in a sack, but there was definitely something strange and evil there."

"What type of sack?" Lara asked.

"Burlap. It was a large brown burlap – "

Lara pointed to the sack behind the drapes. Katie and Meg yelled and ran to the other side of the room. Lara drew her dagger. Flinging back the drapes, she stabbed the sack several times. Then she stopped. She carefully lifted the flap and peered inside. She sprang to her feet.

"Get out of the room," she ordered as she briskly walked over to them.

"What is it?" asked Katie.

"Nothing. It's empty. Get out now."

It was then they heard the hiss, directly above them. Though moments before, the ceiling had been bare, a large black snake with a red underbelly now clung to it. The women quickly jumped back as the snake plopped to the ground. Its body was not smooth, but knotted and twisted. The distorted creature was now between them and the door. It raised its head, allowing them to see its massive size and glowing red eyes. It rose above the frame of the door, and its body was almost as wide as a man's.

"Of course, it's a snake," Meg murmured.

"Is it?" Katie asked.

The creature flickered its tongue.

"Slowly step back," Lara instructed.

Before anyone could move, the creature bared its long fangs and charged at them with lightning speed. Lara quickly forced it backwards with a strong wind while Katie pulled Meg to the window.

"We can climb down!" Katie suggested.

"I can't climb without rope," Meg sputtered.

Despite the wind, the snake began to move towards Lara. Suddenly, it lurched forward, sinking its fangs into Lara's injured side. As Lara fell back, dropping her dagger, Katie grabbed the snake stick leaning against the wall and swung at the creature's head. It did not damage it in the slightest, but it was enough of a distraction. Lara grabbed the dagger, stabbed the snake, then pushed it back with another gust of wind.

Katie helped Lara to the window, but the snake slithered quickly after them. Its movements were precise and fast. Lara created another wind and threw the dagger. It struck the snake near its head and sent it flying back against the wall. It was now pinned but still squirming. The door was no longer blocked, but they didn't dare go near the creature as it screeched and squirmed. Katie yelled for help. Meg tried as well, but no sounds came from her lips. Lara, having no other weapon, grabbed hold of the mirror on the vanity and smashed it to the ground, shattering the glass. She looked up. The snake had somehow molted its skin at an impossible speed. It wrenched itself free just as Alma came running into the room.

"No!" Meg shouted.

The snake stopped in front of Alma, flicked its tongue, then quickly turned its head, disregarding her completely. It sprang towards the other women before getting distracted by the droplets of blood on the floor. It bit into the ground with vigor.

"Alma, get out now!" Lara ordered.

As soon as the girl ran out, Lara created another wind. It picked up the pieces of glass and plunged them into the snake. It writhed in pain on the floor, but was still very much alive. At that moment, Ty came in, having heard Katie's call for help. When he saw the snake, he drew his sword and brought it down on the snake's head. It screeched and tried to strike. Lara sent it back with her wind. While Lara held the beast back from striking, Ty continued to hack at the creature until, after the fourth blow, he succeeded in lopping off its head. The body twitched violently and then gradually became still. Lara exhaled and pushed her dark hair out of her face. Several other knights had now come to investigate the noise.

"Good work, Sir Ty," Lara warmly remarked.

"I extend the same compliment to you," he answered, slightly out-of-breath. "What is going on? I've never seen a snake like that!"

Alma pushed past the knights. She ran into the room and embraced Meg.

"It's a magic snake!" said Katie.

"Kate, quickly go in my bag and wrap me up again," said Lara as she eased herself into a chair. "Do a quick job, just enough to stop the bleeding."

Katie complied, wrapping the bandage awkwardly over Lara's clothes, all while trying to explain to Ty and the others what just happened.

"Lara, we really should take care of your wound," Katie protested.

"There's no time. Just do what you can. If I heard you correctly, you said we'll be under attack again soon."

Just then, there was a commotion outside. One of Katie's bells began to ring. All of the knights except Ty ran out to investigate.

"Not again," Katie sighed.

"That's good enough. Just tie it," Lara stated.

Katie did as instructed. Lara began to run to the door.

"Wait!" said Ty. "You're not well enough to – "

Lara sent another wind, causing Ty to stumble back and giving Lara enough room to pass by. She sprinted out of the room and ran towards the staircase.

"She must be alright," Katie said with a shrug.

"She's so bossy," Ty complained as he hurried to join Lara.

Chapter 17: Lara's Rain

"Fire! Fire! The castle's on fire!"

Lara and Ty heard frantic shouting as they raced down the stairs. There was no fire in the castle foyer, but they could see the smoke and flames from the windows. Lara stopped a knight.

"Is the fire inside the castle?" she asked.

"Not yet," he answered.

She let him go and ran to a window. Ty followed. They saw that most of Katie's courtyard was now aflame. The knights who were attempting to put out the fire were being shot, though Lara could not tell who was shooting the arrows or where they were even coming from. There was too much smoke. Lara clenched her fists and pressed down against the window ledge. She closed her eyes and concentrated.

"I need to get out there," said Ty.

"No. Wait."

"We can't wait, Lara. I need – Is that Killian? Lara, Killian's out there!"

"Shh. Wait."

The sky darkened. Lara raised both her arms then flung them down. A lightning bolt struck a tree, splitting it in half.

"No, come on," Lara murmured.

She lifted her arms again and unclenched her fists. Ty heard the rumbling of thunder. Lara dropped her arms, and a heavy downpour began.

"Now we can go," Lara stated.

Ty leaped out the window, landing easily on the ground. Lara shakily lifted herself up to the ledge. Grunting, she gave up that endeavor and resigned herself to exiting the castle the conventional way. When she reached the door, the fire was already nearly extinguished. The knights, no longer worried about the fire, were kneeling and using their shields to protect themselves from the arrows. Those who had no shields quickly ran back into the castle to retrieve them. Lara scanned the grounds. She spotted Ty and Killian between two large oak trees. Lara ran to them. When Ty saw her coming, he pointed her out to Killian. They both quickly hurried out to meet her and escorted her safely back to the meager shelter the trees provided.

"I told her to stay, but she didn't listen to me . . . again," Ty remarked.

An arrow hit the tree bark near his head. He ducked.

"Lara, they're coming from the wall surrounding Katie's castle," Killian explained. "I think someone must have used magic to make a secret entrance into the outer wall."

Lara glanced up. The arrows did seem to be coming from there. She raised her hand and then pointed to the wall. Lightning struck, causing the stones to explode and sending an unfamiliar soldier flying out.

"You're right," said Lara.

"You can't destroy all of Katie's wall just to get to them," Ty stated.

"If I can reach the wall and find an entrance, I can send people inside to fight."

Ty glanced at Killian, who nodded.

"I don't really understand, but let's do it," Ty said.

Killian whistled and motioned for the other knights to join them. Using their shields, they protected Lara and made their way to the wall. She felt along the stones. Still, the arrows assailed them, either breaking on the impact of their shields and armor or striking the knights. Some men attempted to shoot at the attackers hidden in the wall, but their arrows only struck rocks with no impact on anyone hidden within. The rain continued to pour.

At last, Lara found a way in. She pressed her hands forward, and they disappeared into the stones. She spread her arms apart and instructed the knights to go in. They gladly complied, vanishing into the wall. The arrows ceased as the enemy soldiers were soon dispatched, while the remaining ones attempted to flee by leaving through another entrance. Katie's soldiers began their pursuit while Killian led the injured but reluctant Lara back inside the castle.

Aidan began to chase the retreating enemy, but spied someone riding over the hill in the opposite direction. The stranger rode a white horse speckled with black. Aidan mounted his own horse and gave chase, leaving the rainstorm behind him. As he neared, he saw that the stranger was, in fact, only a boy. Aidan reached forward and grabbed the reins to the boy's horse. The angry lad tried unsuccessfully to swing at him.

"Stop," ordered Aidan. "I just need to question you. Why were you running?"

"You'll get nothing from me!" the boy shouted as he continued swinging wildly.

Aidan caught his arm and stared at him.

"Edwin?"

The boy's look of surprise transformed into a glare. He pushed Aidan's arm away.

"You're one of them?" Edwin asked in disgust.

"Are you part of this? Were you involved in this attack?"

"You'd know that if you hadn't left," Edwin scoffed.

"This is important, Ed. Tell me what's going on? Are you involved?"

"I'm not telling you anything, traitor."

"Tell me, Edwin!"

"Traitor!"

Aidan crossed his arms.

"Then I call upon our bond of friendship."

"Stop!" Edwin protested. "That's not fair, and you know it!"

"We swore to help each other," Aidan reminded him, "and by forest, lake and field of Ellowyn, so named Blackwood – "

"Fine! Stop! Okay," Edwin relented. "Look, Aidan, I'm in the middle of an escape. I've got to go before someone catches me, and if I stay much longer, the man I work for – the captain – he'll get suspicious."

"Then hurry back with me and explain."

"No way! You can't turn me in! You'd break our oath. I'll meet you later. I'll explain myself then," Edwin gave Aidan a distrustful look, "and *you* can explain *yourself*."

"I'm not falling for that."

"There's a forest near here. It's called Ply Forest."

"Pyre Forest."

"Whatever. I'll meet you in the plain between Ply Forest and the river. I'll be there at midnight tonight, no matter what, but you have to let me go now, and you must promise to meet me there alone."

"I'm not an idiot, Ed. You're just going to disappear."

Edwin lifted his chin. He raised his right hand and said, "I swear by the forest, lake, and field of Ellowyn, so named Blackwood, Nahiri, and Grover, that I will be in that plain alone at midnight."

Aidan sighed and raised his hand as well.

"And I swear by your oath, I shall come alone."

They clasped hands, looked to their left, and spat on the ground.

"Now I *really* need to go," Edwin said.

"Well, don't forget your promise," Aidan called as the boy rode off.

Aidan returned alone to the rainstorm at Katie's castle, which was gradually slowing down. He searched for Killian and was told he would find him in the library. He wiped off the mud from his shoes and walked towards the room. He heard Lara's voice and slowed his steps. He took a deep breath and walked on. He peeked inside the library. He saw Lara sitting in a chair. Her wound had obviously been properly treated this time. Killian was pacing with his arms crossed.

"What is the point of possessing magic if I can't use it?" Lara asked Killian.

"You can use it, and you did," he answered. "Don't you think it would be unwise for you to go after them when you need medical attention? I'm sure Katie's knights are capable of catching them all by themselves."

"But they didn't last time. I don't want them to get away."

"Give the knights some credit, Lara."

Killian glanced up and noticed Sir Aidan leaning into the room, still hesitating to enter.

"Yes?" Killian asked.

"I just need to talk to you when you're done," Aidan stammered. "It's not important."

"Go talk to him," said Lara. "I'm fine."

"First, I need to give you something." Killian smiled. "The reason I came here this afternoon was to surprise you with a birthday gift."

"I don't like gifts."

"You'll like this one."

"And it's nowhere near my birthday."

"That's why it's a surprise."

"That's not how that works."

"Don't tell me how it works. Just wait here," he playfully answered.

Killian dashed out of the library. Aidan shifted his feet, uncertain what to say. Lara was perfectly content to let the silence remain unbroken. Fortunately, Killian quickly returned with a large chestnut-colored bag. Lara gave him a skeptical look and opened it, withdrawing a branch covered in small yellow flowers.

"I didn't think there were any left this season," Lara said with a fond smile.

"I knew you would like them."

"What's so special about yellow lilies?" Aidan ventured to ask.

Lara explained, "They're not lilies. They're called 'golden

rain.' When ingested, they cause vomiting, paralysis, bowel excretion, frothing at the mouth, and sometimes death."

Lara embraced Killian.

"Thank you so much," she said.

Aidan stared at the plants in horror. When Killian asked him why he needed to talk to him, it took Aidan a few moments to remember what he was going to say.

Chapter 18: Aidan's Friend

A white owl flew to the lone tree in the plain between Pyre Forest and Lynx River. The branches rustled, and the noise was heard by Edwin, who sat underneath. He looked up, and the owl greeted him with a small "hoo." Edwin stretched his legs then returned to poking the ground with a stick.

At exactly midnight, Edwin heard a horse galloping through the woods, getting closer. Edwin hid behind the tree. Aidan slowed the horse when he reached the clearing. He tied the reins to a low-hanging branch. Edwin stepped out, and Aidan walked towards him.

"You're late," Edwin complained.

Aidan answered once he reached him, "You're early."

"I suppose you're here because you want to know all of their secrets then," Edwin spoke. "All of the political intrigue and secret attacks."

"Lay aside the politics."

"How can I when you wear the armor of the enemy?"

"The main reason I came here, Ed, was to make sure you're okay."

"What about the other reason?"

Aidan paused, not knowing how to answer. He picked up a rock and tossed it into the woods.

"You still have a weak arm," Edwin smirked.

"Do better then."

Edwin picked up a stone and threw it as hard as he could. He smiled as it surpassed the spot where Aidan's landed.

"Have I failed you, Ed?"

Edwin didn't look at him. He picked up another rock.

"You didn't fail me," he said as he threw it.

"I should have stayed and looked after you."

"Well, you told me to come with you, but I thought you were crazy to leave. I still think it was a bad idea."

"I guess you found work though?"

"Don't judge me for that."

"I wasn't. I'm asking."

Aidan picked up another stone and heaved it.

"Fine, I found work," Edwin admitted. "I'm the assistant or errand boy or jolly-knows what else to one of those thugs-for-hire. This one calls himself 'the captain.'"

"What's his real name?"

"It doesn't matter. He's a nobody. You know the type – just a thug. The captain's not your main concern."

"I thought the knights of Callaway caught everyone who attacked the castle."

"You caught the captain's men, but not him. He's always got an extra escape plan, and since the captain's still free, that means I've still got my employment."

"So, who is my main concern if not the captain?"

"There are several players." Ed leaned against the tree and counted on his fingers. "You've got me. I'm lowest of importance. Then you've got the captain's men, but you've captured or killed all of them. Then there's the captain. Above him, you've got the man who hired the captain. This man tells the captain what to do and feeds him information. The captain calls him 'the big money man,' but he let a name slip once."

"What was the name?"

Edwin smiled and chucked a rock.

"Lucius."

"Why would Baron Lucius hire a thug?"

"I wasn't told why, but I have a guess. See, we were hired to kidnap Lady Meg. Then, we'd make it look like someone from Callaway was behind it. I don't know who, but it doesn't really matter who we frame. I'm guessing then that Baron Lucius would pretend to be all insulted and get all huffy at Varden for not controlling his people. Then I guess he'd call off the alliance, and everyone gets to go their separate way."

"I'm not sure it would work out as simply as that."

"Well, you can't blame the baron for trying. I wouldn't want any daughter of mine to marry a king of Callaway."

"It doesn't make sense." Aidan reached down and grabbed a rock. "Why go through the trouble of attacking Duchess Kaitlin's castle?"

"To get Lady Meg. Duh."

"But why not just grab her when she was sleepwalking? When she's already outside the castle walls? Why go through the trouble of taking her every night only to leave her somewhere to be found? They could have kidnapped her then and blamed her disappearance on Duchess Kaitlin."

Edwin stared at him with new-found curiosity.

"Lady Meg sleepwalks?"

Aidan paused mid-throw.

"You didn't know that?"

"No, but you have to tell me now. Come on. I've told you a lot already."

Aidan tossed the rock and answered, "Fine, Lady Meg was sleepwalking. Someone put night-shadow into her perfume or something, and it caused her to have these weird hallucinations and to sleepwalk."

"That's terrible!"

"She would disappear, and someone would find her in

Varden's – King Varden's castle. Apparently, someone named 'Dante' was behind it."

"That dirty snake!"

"It's funny you mention snakes, since he seems to be amassing an army of powerful magic ones."

"Don't play games," Edwin scoffed.

"I swear, it's what I've heard. Besides, I thought Dante was working with your group."

"He's another player in the game, but he may be playing by his own rules. The captain hired him to help us. Much good that did. Some evil witch exposed their hiding place today, and Dante was nowhere to be found afterwards. He used his magic powers to create this weird hiding place in the wall, and then he set fire to the whole courtyard! It was amazing!"

"Right. Amazing."

"If only it hadn't rained."

"Do you know where Dante is now?"

"I can't tell you. The captain is supposed to meet with him tonight to work out a new plan. If it doesn't work, he plans on paying Dante a visit in his not-so-secret hiding place."

"Be careful. He sounds dangerous."

"Dante's got his own informant too. I followed him earlier today before we attacked. He met someone in the woods, but the person rode off before I could get close enough to see them. I thought I saw a dress, but I think now it might have been a cloak."

"Dante's informant wore a dress?"

"I thought so, but now I think I just saw a cape or a cloak or something. Trust me, no female would want to meet Dante alone in the woods. The guy is a creep."

Edwin glanced around nervously.

"I have to go now. I'm supposed to be at hand when the captain meets Dante. Don't follow me."

"I don't suppose I could convince you to – "

"Don't even try. My loyalty lies with Ellowyn. There is something else you can do for me. You can tell me where Lady Meg is."

"Not happening."

"I've helped you enough. Now you need to tell me something useful. I'll find out soon enough anyway."

Aidan gave a nervous cough. He glanced up into the tree. The owl turned its head and looked down at him.

"She's at King Varden's castle right now," he whispered to Edwin. "I doubt she'll stay there tomorrow night, knowing that her father might be behind these attacks."

"Good. That's good to know."

Aidan again tried to convince Edwin to go back with him. He would be safe, even among people of Callaway, but Edwin wanted nothing to do with them. As he ran off into the woods, Aidan tossed a stone into the river. The owl turned its head at the sound of the <<ker-plunk>>, but it remained up in the tree. Only after Aidan mounted his horse and rode off did the owl flap its wings and follow after him.

Chapter 19: A Secret Place

"Okay. Everything's okay," Aidan muttered.

He slowed his horse to a comfortable trot.

"They were going to find out where Lady Meg was staying anyway, so it's not *that* bad you told them."

After another realization, he made a fist and pounded it against the saddle.

"The sleepwalking! I didn't have to tell him that. I though he already knew. Stupid!"

He went to strike the saddle again, but his hand slipped and brushed up against the horse. Aidan's annoyed expression changed to one of contrition.

"Sorry. Sorry," he apologized.

He glanced back at the owl following him.

"You gave away too much information," he chided himself. "She's going to be mad. They say her eyes turn yellow when she's mad, but you know that's not true. She – she's just a normal, regular person. I wish Ty had never told me she was a witch. She's probably nice once you get to know her. Everything will be okay. Probably."

As he rode towards Varden's castle, Aidan could see the outlines of the soldiers positioned on the wall. Beside one of the parapets, he could make out the shape of two people wearing no armor. One was a woman. Lara.

Lara lowered the spyglass.

"Sir Aidan is coming," she said.

"Good," Varden spoke. "I'll go down to meet him. You can stay up here until he's safely in the castle, just to make sure nothing happens. We'll wait for you and Killian to join us in the study. I don't want you to miss anything he has to say."

Lara nodded.

"By the way, I just remembered something. I heard Jerald has been impersonating me."

"I haven't heard anything."

"Well, fortunately, he's been rather unsuccessful. Most everyone knows who he is." Varden sighed. "I'll be happy when Meg and I marry and I can finally ensure Jerald is no longer next-in-line to the throne should anything happen to me."

He studied Lara. She made no reply.

"You don't approve," he observed.

"I didn't say anything."

"You do this motion with your eyebrow when you're not pleased with something."

Lara glanced at him and raised her eyebrow.

"That's not it," said Varden. "Look, Lara, I value your advice."

He waited expectantly.

"Lady Meg is not ready to marry," Lara answered.

"I see," Varden spoke with evident disappointment. "You think she does not care for me?"

"I think she cares a great deal for you. I don't know why since she hardly knows you."

Lara grimaced at how harsh the words sounded, but Varden urged her to continue.

"She's not ready to trust you, and I don't know if you should trust her. She has too many secrets."

"We all have secrets," Varden defended her.

"Yes, that is true."

He nodded.

"Thank you, Lara. I'll meet you in the study."

As soon as he turned and left, Killian walked over to Lara.

"I didn't want to interrupt," said Killian. "You seemed to be having an important discussion. May I have a look?"

Lara handed him the spyglass. He held it up and studied Aidan.

"If Aidan hadn't insisted on traveling alone," Lara remarked, "we could have followed him to make sure he was alright."

"He seemed to do just fine. Besides he had his own off-putting friend, a *fowl* friend, if you will."

"If we had been at this meeting, I could have sent the bird to follow Edwin. Then we would know the location of their hideout."

"Hmm." Killian lowered the spyglass and smiled mischievously. "Care to make a wager?"

"Should I be concerned about your new-found love of gambling?"

"I'll wager that the first thing Aidan says to you is, 'Please don't be mad.' What do you think?"

"I'm not betting."

"Still standing on your principles?" he teased.

"No, he most likely will say that." Lara took the spyglass and had another look. "Just as I thought. He's talking to himself, which means he's nervous. He always says that to me when he's nervous."

"He's only ever nervous around you. You scare the poor boy."

"That's not my fault. Besides, he's also nervous around someone else now."

"Who?"

"A young woman."

"Do tell."

"It's not for me to say. He's riding through the gate now. We should go."

"You're so cruel."

Killian and Lara quietly made their way to the study. Varden and Aidan awaited them. When Aidan saw Lara, he turned to her and said, "Please don't be upset."

"Upset?" Killian noted. "Not mad. You would have won, Lara."

Lara ignored his remark. Aidan explained all that happened by Pyre Forest, leaving nothing out. Since Baron Lucius now appeared even more untrustworthy than before, it was decided that his wife and daughter should be taken somewhere safe. The next morning, Varden managed to speak to both of them, away from the baron. Though he explained the situation and the possible danger, Baroness Isabelle insisted on remaining at King Varden's castle. She was scared, but she was more worried about her husband's displeasure once he discovered she was gone. No amount of persuasion on Varden or Meg's part would change her mind. Meg, however, agreed to go on the condition that Alma accompanied her.

The rest of the day was uneventful aside from the secret plans made by Varden and his trustworthy companions. That night, Varden, Killian, and Lara quietly led Meg and Alma out of the castle. Varden and Killian carried the bags containing Meg and Alma's personal belongings. The moon was out, but Lara hid its brightness behind the clouds. They walked in darkness to the hills near Katie's castle. At one particular hill, they stopped. Lara stepped up to it and held out her hands, which disappeared into the hillside. The hill began to split, creating an opening. Everyone stepped through, and the hill closed behind them.

Meg and Alma looked around in amazement. They were in a quaint kitchen. A door led to the rest of the house which consisted of one small bedroom and a small empty room beside it. Aside from the candles on a shelf, the main light came from the fireplace. A large pot hung over the fire. Some empty bowls and spoons lay on the ground beside it. There were several windows in the kitchen that showed them views from the outside. Katie sat in one of the few chairs at a small table. She stood and set down a book, placing it on top of a large pile of books that covered the table and some of the floor.

"Is this your home?" Meg asked Lara.

"No, it belonged to an old sorcerer. He no longer lives here. I don't know where he is now."

"Will he mind us staying here?"

Lara shrugged.

"Don't worry," said Katie. "He hasn't been here for nearly two years now."

Killian put the bags in the bedroom. Meg and Alma walked in and quietly unpacked some of their things, setting them in a drawer in the wardrobe. Alma pulled out a blue bottle.

"What's that?" asked Meg.

Alma explained with her hands, and Meg nodded. Katie knocked on the open door and leaned inside.

"I made some soup."

Meg and Alma joined the others in the kitchen. Katie filled two bowls with warm soup. Varden, Killian, and Lara were sitting on the floor, searching through the books.

"I'm afraid you can't use the table," Katie pointed out. "We're using that to hold all the books we haven't looked through yet."

"Do all these belong to the sorcerer?" asked Meg.

"No, they're Lara's. She brought them over this afternoon."

"Alma and I can help. What are we looking for?"

"Any information on blood magic," Lara answered without looking up.

"But you said it doesn't exist," Meg pointed out.

"But Dante say it does, so now we're looking," she stated matter-of-factly.

Meg and Alma took the soup and joined them on the floor. Varden offered them chairs, but they politely declined. Katie handed them a small pile of books. Alma sipped some soup while Meg leafed through the pages of a heavy volume of jumbled notes.

"Are these organized in any way?" she asked.

"Yes," Lara answered.

Behind her, Varden and Killian shook their heads.

"They're arranged alphabetically by category," Lara explained.

"Then, I must look under 'B' for blood magic?"

"No, it's probably under 'N' for non-existing magic, or it could be under 'M' for myths."

"I see."

Meg shared a smile with Varden and flipped open the book.

Chapter 20: The Lost Brooch

Meg set down the empty soup bowl. Stifling a yawn, she picked up the book, resuming where she had left. Alma leaned against her shoulder, trying desperately to stay awake.

"Any luck yet?" Varden asked Meg.

She smiled and shook her head. Lara looked up from her book.

"Sorry. I actually found it already," Lara confessed.

Everyone sat up.

"When did you find it?" Killian questioned her.

"Just a few minutes ago. I was too busy reading to tell you."

"Where was it?" asked Meg. "Under 'M' or under 'N?'"

"It was under 'F.'"

Varden's perplexed look coaxed another smile from Meg.

"F?" Varden asked.

"Fables."

"I see."

"What did you find out? Tell us," Katie urged.

"It seems, according to what's recorded, it is rare someone has the ability to use blood magic. It's done when a sorcerer kills an animal, recites a curse, and uses his own blood to revive it."

"Ew," said Katie.

"The animal then craves the taste of blood, but will not attack the sorcerer because it recognizes the smell of the sorcerer's blood as its own. Likewise, the creatures will not attack each other."

"That's a pity," remarked Killian.

"At least they may not be venomous. It bit me with no effects. According to this, the creatures kill by biting their victim and draining them of blood."

"That's gross," Katie spoke. "Snakes don't do that. They either use strangulation or venom and then swallow the prey whole."

"These aren't snakes anymore," Lara reminded her.

"This is so confusing," Katie complained. "We don't even know how much of this is true. A few days ago, you didn't even think they were real."

"Can they be killed?" asked Meg.

"We know first-hand they can be," Lara answered, "but they seem to be more powerful than their previous state. If the sorcerer is killed, perhaps these creatures will die as well."

"We don't even know where Dante is," Varden sighed.

"That's all that's written about blood magic," said Lara. "I don't know anything else."

"I suppose we should get some sleep," said Killian. "It's probably quite late. We can look through the other books tomorrow just in case there's something else."

Killian stood and stretched.

"He chose snakes," Lara mused.

"Well, Callaway has a lot of them," Killian remarked. "They also have a strong sense of smell."

"'Of course, it's a snake.' That's what you said," Lara spoke to Meg.

"What?"

"You said, 'Of course, it's a snake,' the first time we saw it," Lara stated.

"Well, it was a snake, Lara," said Katie. "It was obvious."

Killian looked at Lara with curiosity and resumed his seat on the floor.

"It was obvious, yes," Lara confirmed. She looked back at Meg. "But you were not surprised. You said 'of course,' as though it was a logical revelation, as though it made sense."

"Nothing about it makes sense," Meg answered. "Besides, as Killian said, there are many snakes, and they have a strong sense of smell. If the blood creatures need smell, snakes are a logical choice."

"You know something the rest of us do not," Lara accused her.

"I've told you everything."

"You were cautious when you described your hallucinations. I thought it was because you were scared, but it was because you didn't want to reveal anything that would give you away."

"I think we need to go to bed," Meg stated with a slight laugh. She rose to her feet with her empty bowl.

"We need to know everything," Lara continued. "You don't know what could be useful, what could help us."

"Goodnight," said Meg.

She placed her bowl on top of the other dirty dishes near the dying fire. She started to leave, but immediately halted when she heard Lara's next words.

"Alma is the one behind this."

Meg quickly spun around.

"Have you lost your senses?" Meg asked.

"Lara," Katie began, "I'm sure Alma is not involved in – "

"You were there, Kate," Lara interrupted. "You saw what happened with the creature. It didn't want Alma. It recognized her."

"That's not true," Meg firmly denied. "Dante created the snakes, not Alma."

"Did he?"

"Lara," Varden warned.

Killian held his hand out, motioning to Varden to wait. Lara stood, holding up the book.

"Read it for yourself," she said, shoving it towards Meg. "The creatures don't attack the ones who made them."

Alma slumped down, attempting to hide from everyone's stares, though everyone was mostly staring at Lara.

"Dante brought the snake," Meg argued.

"Dante brought it, but he didn't create it," Lara stated. She pointed at Alma. "The snake wouldn't attack its master."

"Stop it!" Meg ordered. "It's not Alma. She is innocent of everything."

"Alma is the one behind all of this! She's the one using blood magic to create the creatures."

"That's a lie!"

"She is also Dante's informant, and she is the one who tainted your oil with nightshade and caused your hallucinations. This whole time, she has been plotting against us!"

"She has nothing to do with this! Stop throwing out such wild accusations!"

"Then why did the creature ignore her? There's no other explanation!"

"Yes, there is!"

"Then what is it?" Lara demanded.

Meg hesitated, still angry but unwilling to speak farther. She stared at Lara, enraged. Lara stared back, not angry but determined. Everyone else was now looking down, uncomfortable at this exchange. The silence lingered for nearly a minute before Lara spoke.

"There is another explanation," she calmly spoke. "I don't know what it is, but *you* do. You must tell us the truth."

Meg gritted her teeth.

"This is none of your business, Lara. Telling you won't help us."

"Perhaps it won't," Katie answered. She looked up at Meg. "But it may help you. Whatever it is, you can't keep it with you any longer."

Now everyone stared at Meg. Her anger subsided into uncertainty. She stood there, looking like a child who was about to be punished. She looked at Alma, and the girl nodded her head. She pointed to her mouth, then to Lara. Meg sat down in a chair while Lara sat on the floor.

"Fine. It happened years ago," Meg began, "when I was young and foolish. I went sailing on a lake in Ellowyn, Lake Nahiri. Some of the servants were on the boat with me, including Terrence. He . . . he was Alma's brother."

Meg bit her lip and bowed her head. Alma got up and knelt beside her, taking Meg's hand.

"My brooch fell into the water when I leaned over the boat. It was of little value, and I had no personal attachment to it, but I ordered Terrence to jump in and find it. He was just a boy, but he had to listen because he was a servant." Meg sniffed. "It took me no time at all to complain about some other trivial matter and forget all about him. He was just a servant, after all. I thought so little of him, of anyone really."

Varden stood and offered her a handkerchief. She waved it away, wiping her tears with her hand as more trickled down her cheeks.

"We found him some time later. He had drowned. He had this mark on his neck. We . . ." Meg drew in a shaky breath, "We don't have many snakes in Ellowyn, but there are some dangerous ones we call 'water-crawlers.' They float on the surface of water, but they're usually in bogs or swamps, not in lakes. Their bite is paralyzing to humans. Poor Terrence! One of the snakes must have bit him when he swam to the surface, and I was too preoccupied to notice he couldn't move and was slowly drowning."

This time, Meg did take Varden's handkerchief. Her next words were barely audible.

"He found my brooch," she murmured.

No one said a word. No one could find anything reassuring to say. The only sound was Meg and Alma's soft crying. Katie withdrew a handkerchief from her sleeve and quietly wiped her eyes as well. At last, Lara spoke.

"I don't understand. How does that story relate to the current situation?"

Meg sniffed and answered, "I know who Dante is. He . . ." She looked at Alma, who nodded and squeezed her hand. "His name is Dannel. He's Terrence's father, Alma's father. Perhaps that's why the snake ignored her, because she shares Dannel's blood."

Lara and Varden exchanged a glance.

Meg continued, "After what happened at the lake, Dannel was understandably distraught. He accused me of being a thoughtless, selfish creature, which was true."

"Perhaps then, but not now," Varden spoke.

"My father was going to punish Dannel for his disrespectful comments. Dannel was a servant, and servants shouldn't insult their betters, after all. The next day, Dannel was gone. He left, and I never saw him again – until a few months ago. I saw him in my dreams. Well, I thought they were dreams, brought on by a guilty conscience."

"Wait," said Killian, "When Dannel left years ago, did he know about Alma? Did he leave her behind?"

Alma nodded. She pointed to herself, brought her hands together, then separated them. She gestured some more, pointing to her scarred face.

"Alma and her father were not close," Meg interpreted. "He loved Terrence but not Alma because of Alma's face and because he blamed her for her mother's death. Her mother died shortly after giving birth."

Meg and Alma continued providing details of their life well into the night. Lara went to sleep first. First, she apologized to Alma for falsely and knowingly accusing her of conspiring against them. Alma forgave her graciously, and Lara retired to the empty room with a pillow and blanket. Katie soon joined Lara. Alma went to the bedroom, and Killian slept in the far corner of the kitchen. Meg and Varden stayed up talking until nearly morning. Meg found she had much to say, and she felt a tremendous sense of relief at finally allowing herself to trust someone, besides Alma, of course. Meg felt accepted and perhaps a sense of belonging that she never felt before.

Chapter 21: The Hunt

Lara knelt down in the grass as a grey cat approached. She untied the note from around its neck. As she read it, she stroked the cat's back. It purred happily until Lara stopped, hissing in displeasure when Lara turned to go.

"What? I can't scratch your back all day."

The cat flicked its tail and darted away. Lara walked back into the hill. Inside the kitchen, Meg, Varden, Alma, and Katie were playing a card game. They had already looked through the rest of the books in a fruitless attempt to find more information on blood magic. Killian was cooking dinner.

"Did you really use a cat to deliver a message?" asked Katie.

"Killian said I shouldn't use birds," Lara answered.

"That's not what I said," he argued. "I said that your birds are not always discreet when they follow someone. They deliver messages just fine."

"May I see the note?" asked Varden.

"Ty says things are getting out of hand," Lara stated as she handed it to him.

"How so?" asked Meg.

"Jerald is trying to assume as much power as he can, and Baron Lucius is threatening to wage war, accusing King Varden of kidnapping you."

"But I left him a note," said Meg, "and my mother knows I left willingly."

"One day," sighed Varden. "I've been gone one day, and complete chaos ensues."

He had to leave. They all knew from the start Varden could not stay long, but their disappointment was still evident. Meg's even more so. Once Varden returned to his castle, he quickly reversed any damage Jerald had done. The matter with Baron Lucius was not so easily remedied. Though Varden stated that Meg was hiding for her own safety and of her own volition, Lucius dismissed both Varden's words as well as Meg's note. He continued fuming and hurling accusations.

Varden did not care if the baron was in a foul mood and made little effort to appease him. He did not bother asking Lucius's wife to corroborate his story, for Lucius would most likely ignore her. Varden didn't trust him and was determined to do everything in his power to keep Meg safe. He sensed the baron's restlessness, anticipating something would happen that night at the castle.

Varden was only partially correct, for the nocturnal disturbance did not occur at his castle, but at Ty's. Ty was awoken by servants who reported an unusual theft. All of Ty's hounds were missing . . . again. Ty questioned them, and they reluctantly admitted the hounds went missing the previous night, but since they returned an hour later, the servants had not bothered mentioning this to Ty. The unsuspecting Ty had no idea that his hounds were now in the hands of Dante. Dante joined the captain in the woods near Katie's castle. Edwin stood behind the captain, squirming uncomfortably at the growling, barking dogs. The captain yanked the leashes away from Dante.

"This better work tonight, Dante," he threatened.

"It will."

"That's what you said last night," said Edwin.

"Shut up, boy," the captain ordered. He turned back to Dante. "That's what you told us last night. You're testing my patience. I'm not dealing with these mutts again for nothing."

"It was not the right time," Dante explained. "Marguerite must not have used the potion last night, but I have a feeling she will tonight. Now go. I need to cast the spell."

The captain and Edwin went deeper into the woods. Dante closed his eyes.

Is tonight the night? Only fate will tell me. I thought it would not be so soon, but I am ready.

At the cottage in the hill, everyone awoke with a start. An awful smell permeated the home. Everyone congregated in the kitchen, coughing and gagging.

"What is that?" Katie choked.

"It smells like something rotting," Killian complained.

Alma nodded and coughed.

"It smells like hawthorn," Lara answered. "It sometimes has a smell similar to rotting flesh."

Katie stood near Meg and gagged.

"Meg, I think it's something to do with you."

Alma sniffed and then pointed to Meg's hair. Meg grasped several strands and held them under her nose. She grimaced in agreement.

"What did you put in your hair?" questioned Lara.

"Just some oil, but it didn't smell like this when I put it in."

Alma ran back into the bedroom.

"You're not supposed to put oil in your hair," said Lara.

"This is a different one. It doesn't have nightshade."

Alma returned with a blue bottle of oil. She opened it and handed the bottle to Lara. Lara smelled it and went into a coughing fit. Meg sniffed it as well.

"You need to wash your hair," Lara stated.

"I don't understand. It didn't smell that way earlier," she said.

"What's happening?" Katie asked with worry.

A dog howled in the distance. Killian ran to the kitchen window, while Meg and Alma went into the bedroom to find the soap.

"Lara! I see hounds. We need to go."

Meg dumped the basin of water over her head and grabbed the soap.

"Even if they can track us here, they won't be able to get inside, will they?" asked Katie.

"If someone has magic, they can enter. Let's go. Take the soap with you."

Lara set the blue oil bottle on the table, but Katie picked it up and carried it with her. Alma tried to help Meg, who was desperately scrubbing her head with soap. They rushed outside. Seeing the hounds running towards them, they ran down the opposite side of the hill towards the woods. Five dogs soon surrounded them, growling and baring their teeth. Lara waved her hands over her head. The dogs ceased growling and ran off. Lara and the others continued running.

"Way to go, Lara!" said Meg.

"They'll be back," Lara warned. "Then, whoever is using them to track us will find us."

As they reached the forest, they heard the howling dogs again. Killian glanced back and saw three men on horseback following the hounds.

"Lara," said Katie, "if they're tracking Meg with this smell," she held up the bottle, "we can pour it on ourselves and split up. Then, they won't know who to follow."

Lara snatched the bottle.

"That's almost a good idea," Lara remarked.

The captain led the chase, following the dogs closely. He grinned in anticipation of finally achieving his elusive goal and then at last receiving the full payment. The captain, Edwin, and Dante rode into the woods. Suddenly, the dog pack began to separate, so they followed the dogs as best they could. Some of the hounds chased after birds. Others barked at squirrels up in the trees. The captain yelled at them, cursing their stupidity. After chasing the dogs around in circles for over an hour, he at last had to give up when he heard Ty's knights approaching. Meg was long gone. The captain eluded the knights and met with Edwin. Dante was nowhere to be found.

Chapter 22: The Stranger

"Dante! Let me in!" the captain bellowed. "You've got to come out sometime!"

The armor on the captain's arm clanked against the rock as he banged against the boulder. Edwin stood behind him with closed eyes. His head slowly dropped then quickly jerked back up as his eyes few open. He cleared his throat and shuffled his feet.

"Stop squirming," the captain ordered, temporarily ceasing his clanging to scold the boy.

"I can't help it, Captain. I'm tired. We were out all night."

"Exactly! It's morning now, and when the sun's up . . ." the captain jabbed his finger in his direction, ". . . you're up."

"Yes, Sir."

A strong gust of wind burst from the rock, knocking them both down. Edwin gaped in surprise. Dante calmly emerged, cloaked in a black, musty hood. The captain huffed in anger and stood. Edwin remained on the ground, too weary to put in the effort to stand.

"None of your plans have worked, Dante!" The captain drew his sword and pointed it at him. "It's time to pay your debt."

At that moment, a large creature shot out from the rock and latched onto the captain's arm. Its fangs pierced the armor and sank into flesh. Another snake creature emerged. Then another. Edwin watched in horror, shaking but too petrified to run, too scared to think of anything other than the terrible sight before him. The captain screamed and fell to the ground as the creatures covered his body and consumed him. Soon, they began to slither quickly towards Edwin, who was still shaking and still unable to get up.

"It's time to pay the debt," Dante spoke.

The words seemed to snap Edwin out of his haze. He scrambled to his feet and fled. As he ran, Edwin remembered the horses he and the captain rode. He looked around, but it was too late. They were already running away. He had no chance of catching them. Edwin ran through the woods, the creatures close behind him. He could not help but look back as he ran, and each time he did, the creatures came closer. The front of their bodies were raised. Edwin heard their hissing draw nearer and nearer. He felt the slight flickering of a tongue on his neck, and knew in a moment, it would devour him.

He heard a commotion behind him and chanced a look. The creatures had caught an unfortunate deer. They were distracted, but the distraction might not last long. Edwin sprinted onward. At last, he reached the edge of the forest. He stopped for a quick breath, panting and leaning against a tree. He saw one of the creatures still followed. It bore no signs of fatigue. Edwin looked around for any chance of escape. He spied a dark-skinned man slowly walking on the road away from him. He was far away, but Edwin thought he saw the man carried a sword along with his satchel. Edwin called out, but the man didn't hear. He glanced back once more at the creature and found the motivation to continue running.

He raced towards the man on the road. Edwin yelled, but barely, for he was nearly out of breath. The man seemed to hear and turned around. Edwin flailed his arms and glanced behind. The creature was now out of the forest, slithering towards him, in full view of the man. It was too late. The man would see it now and run away.

Edwin was too weary to run further. He drew a dagger and held it out. He couldn't keep his hand steady as the creature rushed towards him. He tried to stab it, but missed. The creature latched onto his leg. Edwin heard something snap. He cried out, fell, and dropped the dagger. The beast raised its head and lunged at Edwin's throat.

A sword struck the creature before it could bite his neck. Edwin looked to his left and saw the man standing beside him. The creature's head was still intact. It charged angrily at the man. He caught it and held it away. The strong creature began to break free of his hold when suddenly, it burst into flames. It screeched while the man held it firmly in his grasp, unaffected by the fire. When at last it stopped moving, the flames disappeared. The man released the creature, and it hit the dirt road with a heavy thud.

The man knelt down beside Edwin.

"Don't worry," he said. "I'm not – I won't hurt you."

He retrieved a cloth from his satchel. He quickly wrapped it around Edwin's bleeding leg.

"It seems to be broken."

The man picked up several sturdy sticks and tied them to Edwin's leg to keep it straight.

"What kind of animals are they?" Edwin asked as he cried in pain.

"I was hoping you would know. There's more than one?"

"So many! Dante must be controlling them!"

"Who is Dante?"

"Some crazy, creepy, insane sorcerer!" Edwin glanced nervously at the man and quickly added, "But I'm sure not all sorcerers are crazy."

The man gave him a friendly smile.

"This Dante must have used blood magic," the man mused. "Would you mind showing me where the creatures came from?"

"No way! Are you crazy?"

"Please, it's important," he pleaded. "Other people could be in danger. I will not – I won't let any harm come to you."

"No! I'm not going back there! *You* can run away, but I can't!"

"I saw a horse run by a minute ago. You could ride that."

"That horse is long gone, Mister."

The man put his fingers in his mouth and whistled. Edwin shook his head in disbelief.

"They aren't trained to come when you whistle, and why would it listen to you? There's no way it could even hear that."

The sound of hoofprints soon disproved Edwin's critiques. He looked behind and saw the captain's horse galloping towards them. Edwin closed his eyes. He was overwhelmed by the pain in his leg and the terrible realization that he might again be in the hands of a sorcerer.

Chapter 23: Escape from the Tower

Baroness Isabelle set down her hairbrush at the sound of knocking. She opened the door to her daughter.

"Marguerite, you're back? I thought you were planning to remain hidden for at least a few weeks. Come in."

"We had to change our plans early this morning."

Meg stepped inside. The room was cluttered with several large chests. Lucius had placed them there, for he had not wanted them taking up space in his own room. Isabelle closed the door and embraced her daughter.

"Well, I'm glad to see you. You're the only person who makes this stay bearable. Your hair is wet. Did you wash it?"

"I did. This morning, in the stream, as we were trying to run."

"What?"

Meg sat down in a chair and said, "We all arrived at Varden's castle a few hours ago. I was too weary to dry it off. I simply wanted to sleep."

"Why on earth were you washing your hair in a stream?"

Meg shrugged.

"It had a terrible smell."

"Well, I don't smell anything." Isabelle sat down across from her. "I didn't know you came back. You see where your father put me." She gestured around the circular room. "It certainly wasn't King Varden's idea to put me in a tower like some forlorn princess. Your father wanted me to be out of his way, which is fine by me, but why should I have to stay here? It's too cramped, and I'm so far removed from everything. It takes me forever to walk down all the stairs. How many steps are there? A hundred?"

"Two hundred and sixty-two."

"Well, there you have it. Also, I have one window in this whole room – one. That's why it's so dark in here. The window is not even facing the right direction. It looks out toward the back of the castle. Who wants to see the rear?"

Meg traced her fingers along the seam of the chair as her mother complained.

"Are you feeling well, Marguerite?" Isabelle asked with concern.

Meg looked up and asked, "Are you Dante's informant?"

Isabelle sat back in shock. Her face paled and mouth dropped open. Meg swallowed and continued her query.

"Are you the one who poisoned my oil with nightshade?"

"Marguerite," Isabelle gasped. "No! Why? Why would you think that?"

"Because you gave Alma the blue bottle of oil for my hair, the bottle that contained hawthorn and magic, the one that was used to track me last night."

Isabelle stood and passionately refuted, "I never gave Alma anything! If something happened last night, I had no part in it! You need to talk to Alma and find out the truth! How could you think so poorly of me?"

Isabelle turned away, visibly distressed.

"Even if I question Alma," Meg replied, "it would be of little consequence. I can't tell when she is lying, because in all the years I've known her, she's never lied." Meg paused. "I can, however, tell when you are."

Isabelle turned around, looking nearly as hurt as Meg.

"Why did you do this?" Meg entreated her. "Why? Don't you know all of the pain you caused me by doing this? And now, you've put others in danger."

"It's your father. It's him! You know how he treats me. Every day, his words wear me down, draining me of life. You are getting married and leaving him, but what about me? I'm still trapped."

"I told you I would help you! I promised. As soon as you said the word, I would help you go and move in with your sister and brother-in-law. They are kind people, and they have offered to help. Why wouldn't you let us help you?"

"It wouldn't work." Isabelle shook her head vehemently. "No, you know it wouldn't work."

"It would!"

"I would have to come back. No, I had to be rid of him."

Meg made no reply. She stood, her face filled with disbelief. Isabelle wrung her hands and looked away.

"I had to be rid of him," Isabelle repeated. "I had to, but I was too . . . *weak* . . ." she spat out the word," . . . too weak to do it myself. I met Dante when I was riding. You know your father doesn't really care if I ride alone. Dante found me, and he told me he would deal with Lucius as long as I did everything he told me."

"You poisoned your own daughter."

"It wasn't poison. It was nightshade, as you said."

"You made me think I was going mad!"

"I told you that you were not. How many times did I say you were perfectly fine? That they were only dreams?"

"Why didn't you let me help you? Why did you enlist the help of *him*?"

"Because I didn't want to run away. Don't you understand? I wanted Lucius dead."

Isabelle covered her mouth and sat on the edge of her bed, shaking.

"You trusted a stranger in the woods more than me," Meg accused her., "and it nearly cost me my life. You have endangered so many people now."

"No, only Lucius! Nothing would happen to you. Dante promised. I only did what I thought was right. You'll see. You'll understand, and then you'll agree with me." She grasped her daughter's arm. "You're just tired right now. Why don't you just go and get some sl- "

"Don't even say it!"

A ringing bell interrupted their argument. It was not the peaceful chime of the cathedral bells but the loud gong of the castle one. Meg looked out the window. She saw knights racing across the courtyard towards the front. She left her mother's chambers and rushed out to the tower stairs. She peered out one of the windows that faced the front of the castle. Dozens of snake creatures littered the courtyard, attacking the knights.

Meg heard her father coming up the stairs, talking to several knights. Lucius insisted he had to go to the tower to protect his wife and child. The knights escorted him up and took Meg back inside, despite her protests. The knights shut the door and remained outside to stand guard.

"What's going on?" asked Isabelle.

"What do you think?" Lucius snapped. "We're under attack!"

"I didn't see the captain anywhere," Meg ventured.

"Neither did I," Lucius answered. "I don't know where he is or where he's gotten those – "

Lucius cut himself short and clamped his mouth shut.

"It's not the captain who is behind this," said Meg. "A sorcerer made those creatures and is now attacking us. He's here for me because he wants revenge."

"How do you know he's here for you?" Lucius questioned.

"Because he tried to find me last night. I am the reason he's here. I have to go out and find him."

"Marguerite!" Isabelle cried. "You can't leave! Not while we are under attack!"

"The attack won't stop until he has what he came for. I don't want people to die because of me."

Lucius rested his hands on Meg's shoulders.

"You do what you have to do," he said.

"Lucius!"

"Shut up, woman! Do you want us all to die?"

Lucius opened the door, but the knights would not allow Meg to leave, though Lucius yelled at them and waved his dagger in their faces. Lucius slammed the door. Meg told him she could climb out the window, but only if she had rope. Lucius brightened at the suggestion. He eagerly dug through one of the large chests and produced a long, thick rope. It reached one hundred and fifty feet, just long enough to reach the ground after securing it to the bed frame. Isabelle was helpless to prevent this reckless plan. Meg carefully managed to climb down. The knights, either rushing past or standing guard in the back, were too preoccupied to notice her. She ran out the back gate. The sky grew dark, and the ground began shaking.

"Dante!" Meg called out. "Dannel!"

She ran in search of him, suspecting he must be near. She at last saw him in the village square. Amidst the panicked villagers who either ran or hid, Dante stood motionless. She boldly ran up to him.

"Stop this!" she ordered. "I know you're here for me. I know you want revenge. You can take me, but leave them alone."

Dante ignored her. He knelt down and placed his hands on the ground, which began to shake. Meg pulled on his arm. The tremors ceased.

"Stop! Dannel, I'm the one who killed Terrance. Kill me and leave! The time to do that has come! The time is now!"

Dante stood up.

"You're right," he spoke. "The time is now."

Dante reached into his cloak. He pulled out a handkerchief, and Meg once again inhaled the foul scent.

Chapter 24: Fraying

Lightning struck the castle wall, shattering the rocks.

"Lara! You hit the wall!" Ty yelled.

"That's not me," she answered.

Ty's blade connected with one of the creatures a second time, at last chopping it in two.

"Can't you redirect his lightning strikes?"

"I can't do five things at once, Ty."

Lara held both hands in front, sending a wind against the creatures. It wasn't strong enough to push them away, but enough to slow them down.

"This isn't working!" Ty shouted. He swung his sword at another, but this time missed. "They're climbing over the walls. There are too many of them."

The knights struggled as they fought the powerful creatures. Lightning struck the castle, hitting one of the towers. Lara raised her arm and sent a lightning bolt of her own. It hit one of the creatures. It jittered but still advanced. Lara struck it with lightning again. It convulsed once more then dropped. Lara repeated this against the others until the ground began to shake again. She placed her hands down to try to stop it.

"We need more of your lightning bolts!" Ty shouted.

"If I stop, this whole castle might collapse on all of us!" she answered.

The castle swayed back and forth. Two of the towers crashed onto the ground before Lara managed to steady the quaking. The tower that contained Lucius and Isabelle leaned backwards. Before they could escape down the stairs, lightning struck the tower, completely obliterating the top. The knights who were guarding the door were trapped under the rubble. Lucius and Isabelle were not so fortunate. Part of the wall was no longer intact. They clung to the sides of what remained. Isabelle grasped at the rope, and Lucius did the same. The tower creaked and leaned even more, causing them to fall over the edge. Were it not for the rope they desperately clung to, they would have surely perished. They wrapped their legs around the rope. Isabelle was nearest the top, and Lucius was several feet below her.

"Isabelle! You're in the way!" he yelled.

"I can't climb! I don't know how!"

"Then get out of the way so I can!"

"Lucius! I can't move!"

Lucius reached down and menacingly withdrew his dagger.

"You can, and you will!"

"Baroness! Baron!" Killian called.

They looked over and saw Killian leaning out a window of

the tower stairs. The rest of the stairs were blocked, and he had gone up as far as he could. He climbed out the window and began making his way up the side of the tower, deftly climbing even without the use of a rope.

"Just hang on! I'll reach the top soon and pull you both up!" he yelled over to them.

Lucius looked back at Isabelle.

"You're lucky this fool is here to help us," he growled.

Isabelle stared down at him, making no reply. Recklessly, she reached down and snatched the dagger, nearly losing her grip on the rope. She glared at Lucius, who just looked back in confusion. Isabelle gritted her teeth, raised her hand, and began cutting the rope.

"What are you doing?!" Lucius yelled.

Isabelle hastily slashed the blade across the rope above her. It was quickly fraying. Lucius grasped her foot.

"We're both going to fall, you idiot!"

"Stop!" Killian shouted.

He had now reached the top. He rushed over to the baroness. Lucius climbed up and grabbed her arm. Killian reached out to her just as she wrenched free of Lucius's grip and made one last attempt. The dagger made a final cut, and the rope split. Killian reached for her, but she made no effort to grab him. His arms were a moment too late. He could do nothing but watch the baron and baroness fall to their deaths. The ground shook briefly again, causing Killian to nearly lose his balance. He stood and went to dig out the trapped knights.

On the ground, Aidan spotted someone riding towards the front gate. The horse weaved around the creatures and jumped over the wall rubble. As the stranger rode closer, Aidan saw Edwin was hanging on behind him. Aidan rushed over as the stranger dismounted.

"Edwin! What happened?" Aidan turned to the man. "Do I know you?"

Before he could reply, a creature lunged towards them. Aidan rushed forward, but the stranger was faster. The man grabbed it, holding onto it until it burst in flames. He let it fall to the ground. Two more creatures approached, but they were struck by lightning and briefly halted their advance. The man turned and saw Lara standing behind them. They stared at each other, but only for a moment. He turned back to face the creatures. Lara went and stood beside him. As the man created more fire, Lara made a wind behind him, pushing the flames from his hands onto the creatures. They set the two creatures on fire, as well as all the remaining ones. Once they were all dispatched, Lara sent a rain to quell the stray flames. Only then did she turn to the man and embrace him.

"I missed you so much," Lara spoke. "Mendel, why were you away for so long?"

"I'm sorry," he said. "I was – I had my own monsters to fight."

Killian spotted them hugging and hurried over.

"Mendel!" He grabbed him and pulled him into a fierce hug.

"You're back!"

"Not to stay, but I'm here to visit," Mendel clarified. "I'd like to help with whatever mess we're in now."

"Only if you promise to be careful," Lara cautioned.

"We can't find Lady Meg," said Killian. "I think Dante may have taken her."

"Dante?" asked Mendel. "Is this – Is Dante the crazy and creepy sorcerer?"

"You know him?" asked Lara.

Mendel glanced over at Edwin. Aidan was assisting him off the horse.

"No," Mendel said, "but I might know where he is."

Chapter 25: Flight

Meg heard the sound of gushing water. She opened her eyes and sat up. She was lying on rocks in a large crevice behind a waterfall. She looked around and nearly jumped. She wasn't alone. She stood facing Dante.

"Alright, get on with it," she ordered.

Dante removed his hood.

"Get on with what?"

"Killing me. Isn't that why you brought me here? To drown me? To get revenge for your son? Go on then."

Dante smiled and shook his head.

"Terrance was meant to drown."

"What? No, it was a terrible accident due to my negligence."

"It was fate. It wasn't an accident." Dante ran his hand along the rocks. "It needed to happen. His death led us to this. I now have the power to overthrow all."

"And replace them with whom?"

Dante shrugged.

"That's not for me to decide."

"You can't overthrow everything and not have a plan! How many innocent people are going to die as you seek vengeance on the world?"

"I have no idea. I knew you would refuse to see the truth, but I'll give you one more chance before I allow my Nahiri to feast on you and your intended."

"My intended?"

"Shh. Listen."

Dante pointed to the rocks behind them. Meg stepped closer. A man was yelling and pounding against the stones.

"Varden? Where is he?"

"He is trapped inside. Oh, you can try, Marguerite, but you cannot go into the stones. You do not possess my powers."

"What do you want?"

"I want you to understand. That is all. If you understand, I'll make sure your death is last." Dante stepped closer. "Just tell me the truth about Terrance's death."

Meg glanced away and answered, "Fine. You're right. Terrance's death was fate. It was necessary for him to die so that you could become the most powerful sorcerer in the world."

Dante frowned.

"You're lying. I can tell."

"Yes," Meg admitted. "Dannel, I'm sorry for his death. I

know I can't make it right, but please kill only me and no one else."

"You will die, but . . ." he put his hand into the rock, " . . . so will King Varden."

Dante pulled him out and flung him to the ground. Meg dropped down and grabbed his hand.

"Jerald?" she said in surprise.

"What?" asked Dante.

"I'm not Varden!" Jerald cried. "I told you! I'm Jerald!"

Dante looked at Meg.

"That's not Varden?"

"No, this is his cousin."

"He told me he was King Varden."

"I lied! Okay? I didn't mean it!" Jerald sputtered. "I promise I'll never do it again!"

Dante turned his head at the sound of screeching.

"What is going on out there?"

He jumped into the water and swam away. Jerald started to jump, but Meg stopped him and pointed out the creatures floating on the water. Dante lifted his head up and saw people at the entrance of his secret hiding place. They were setting his creatures on fire! He quickly swam to the shore.

Very well. Let them all awaken.

"Creatura sanguinis, vita est vita tua!" he yelled.

He clenched his fists and repeated it over and over again. Hundreds more creatures appeared, popping up from both the ground and the water.

"Lara, how many are there?" asked Varden.

"I don't know. We only need to kill him," she answered.

Mendel focused on creating the fire while Lara provided a strong wind, incinerating the creatures. The knights fought as best they could, hacking away and trying to gain some ground. A creature not as big as the others managed to slither past undetected. It bit Lara before she had a chance to kill it. She grabbed it and flung it away.

"I hate these things," Lara muttered. She spread the flames out further. "Why do they always bite *me*? And in the same place?"

The sky thundered overhead, and a few raindrops fell.

"Lara, we don't want it to rain!" Ty shouted. "That will put out the fire!"

"I know that, Ty."

The light trickling began to grow more intense.

"So, stop making it rain!"

"Stop blaming me for the storms, Ty!"

The rain soon made the flames useless, so Lara and Mendel used lightning instead. However, they still were not advancing.

Varden warned, "We need to break through soon to reach Dante before he kills Meg."

A bolt of lightning shot towards them. Lara held up her hands. She re-directed it to hit the creatures, falling to the ground as she did. She quickly got up as a creature charged towards her. She jumped away, but it wasn't trying to get her at all. Instead, it drove its head into the ground, engulfing the droplets of Lara's blood on the grass. Lara stared at it a moment then glanced at Mendel. He didn't understand what she was thinking. He rarely did. Lara struck the snake with lightning and continued fighting.

"I have to reach Dante, but I don't know how," she admitted.

"I don't suppose you have any spare deer," Mendel asked.

"Deer? What do you mean?"

Mendel hit three creatures at once and answered, "Edwin said the deer – the snakes ate the deer instead of him while he was running."

"Wait. It's not just human blood? They'll go after any blood?"

"Yes." Mendel glanced at her. "Lara, no! Don't send any deer in here! That's suicide for them!"

"I know. Wait here."

Lara ran through the boulder guarding the entrance. Mendel heard her whistling. Suddenly, an enormous flock of black crows burst through the boulder. They flew over the creatures, just out of reach. The creatures reached up to try and grab them. Now aimed with distractions, Varden's group charged through, covering more ground as they searched for Meg and Dante.

Meg looked down at the creatures below her. She grasped onto the slippery rocks and looked up at Jerald.

"Jerald! I can't climb as fast as you can. Could you please help me?"

"Don't worry," he said without looking down. "Stay there. I'll get help."

Jerald made his way to the top and began to run towards Varden's group. A creature spotted him immediately, forcing him to run the other way. Meg continued to struggle. One of the creatures was following. Although the creature was far below her, it was moving much faster than she was. She glanced into the lake below, but more creatures were there as well, as if anticipating her fall. The creature slithering up to her was abruptly hit by lightning. It fell, but Meg also lost her grip. She desperately tried to maintain her hold.

Ty, who was ahead of everyone else, raced past the creatures and climbed up the rocks beside the waterfall. The creatures lunged at him, but Ty swatted them with his sword and continued climbing. When it became too steep for him to climb with one hand, he sheathed his sword and hurried to Meg. He reached out for her hand.

"Lara! Send a lightning strike there!" Killian yelled, pointing to Ty and Meg.

"I can't! I might hit them! Ty!"

Ty yelled in pain. A creature was latched onto his arm. His other arm was holding onto Meg. He tried to bang the creature against the rocks without losing his balance. Several others slithered towards them.

"Ty, you have to let go of me," Meg said.

"You're going to fall."

"And you will too if you can't fight them! Let go! I order you! I need someone to tell my mother I forgive her!"

But Ty refused to release his hold. Killian was running towards them, but he could not reach them in time. Just before the other creatures attacked, Lara sent another bolt of lightning. It struck the creature on Ty's arm as well as the surrounding rocks. The creature fell, but Ty also lost his grip. He and Meg fell backwards, down towards the ugly beasts below.

Just before their bodies reached the vicious fangs, they disappeared. A moment later, two hawks flew up and away to safety.

Chapter 26: By Her Hands

Lara at last spotted Dante, slinking along near the waterfall on the other side of the lake. She killed another creature and rushed towards him. Before she could reach him, Jerald burst out from behind a bush and grabbed Lara's arm.

"Lara! You need to take me back to the castle!"

"Not now, Jerald! Get out of the way!"

She pushed him, but Jerald clung to her.

"No! I order you to protect me! Take me back! Take me back now!"

Lara swiftly dealt with Jerald and continued running towards Dante. He saw her coming and stopped, waiting for her.

We must deal with this insolent nuisance.

He removed his black cloak and threw it down. He brushed away his scraggly hair which, soaked from both the lake and the ongoing rain, stuck to his face.

"I don't know who you are," he shouted, "but you are fighting destiny. Give up."

As more creatures came towards Lara, she swiftly struck

them down with lightning. She sent a bolt at Dante, but he easily re-directed it away from him.

"You cannot hit me with lightning," he said.

Lara didn't stop running. Once she got closer, she pulled out a dagger and threw it. Dante caught it. He tossed it into the lake. He sent Lara back with a strong gust of wind.

"You cannot stab me either."

Lara sent her own gust of wind, but not at Dante. She pushed the storm clouds away from them and towards the other side of the lake.

"I can at least make it stop raining," she said.

Dante looked at her, somewhat amused.

"What are you going to do? Set me on fire? You can't do that either."

Lara grabbed another dagger. She made large cuts on the palms of her hands then threw the blade at Dante. He rolled his eyes and caught it, but did not have time to stop Lara from charging into him. She knocked him to the ground, placed her hands around his neck, and pressed down. Dante rolled over and on top of her. Lara struck his face hard with both hands and dug her nails in, but Dante put his hands on her neck. Lara moved her hands from his face, her blood smearing across as she did so. She grabbed his hands, struck Dante with her knee, then rolled free. She stepped away from him. Dante sat up in a kneeling position and shrugged.

"I told you. You cannot kill me."

More creatures advanced towards Lara.

"I don't plan to," she spoke.

As one of them lunged, Lara caught it. She hefted it towards Dante with all her strength. He shook his head.

"They do not attack me," he explained. "They are my – aah!"

The creature was latched to his hand. Dante tried shaking it off. Lara made her fire and scorched any creatures that came near her while several more came after Dante. He stood and began to run, but they quickly overcame him. They sank their fangs into his hands, his face, his neck, anywhere Lara had left her blood. While Lara fought them, Dante was consumed by them. They eventually stopped when no traces of Lara remained, but it was too late. Dante managed to crawl to the lake, reaching out to touch the water once more before he breathed his last.

The creatures all convulsed, shrinking and transforming before dropping dead as ordinary snakes. Killian and Varden ran over to Lara.

"Is Mendel alright?" she asked.

"Mendel? Yes, he's fine," Varden assured her. "He got one bitemark. That's all."

"Good," said Lara.

She knelt down on the grass. Killian worked quickly to bandage her hands. The other knights began walking around the lake, in search of Meg. Varden picked up Dante's cloak and draped it over his body.

"We still haven't found her," Varden explained to Lara. "Do you think she's still alive?"

"She's still alive. I saw her," said Killian. "I'm sure Lara can find her, but do you mind giving us a moment to talk?"

"Of course not," said Varden.

He stepped away. Killian finished wrapping her hands and gently kissed Lara's fingertips.

"At least Mendel is here. We need someone with magic to get us back through the boulders. Killian, you said you would love me without magic. Is that still true?"

Killian caressed the side of her face.

"You know it's true."

"It could take years for me to learn again. I'm not even sure if I can."

"I love you, Lara," Killian replied. "I love you. That is all."

He bent his head and gave her a sweet kiss as his hands ran through her hair. Lara tugged his neck, pulling him closer. At last, she pulled away and stood. She looked up at the black crows still circling above. She whistled, and sent them away. Lara continued whistling until two hawks flew to her. One had an injured wing. After they landed near Lara's feet, she held out her hands and closed her eyes, concentrating. The others drew near to watch. Slowly, the hawks faded, eventually disappearing altogether. Then, Ty and Meg gradually appeared in their place. Varden embraced Meg, while Lara offered Ty assistance in tending to his arm.

"That was an interesting experience," Meg mused.

"At least you were a bird and not a mouse," Varden answered.

"A mouse?"

"I'll tell you later."

"Well, now that Dante is gone, I suppose our wedding is still planned for next week?" Meg smiled.

Varden smiled back. He took her hand, kissed it, and answered.

"No."

Meg's eyes widened.

"No? You're breaking the engagement."

"No, not unless you want to," Varden answered. "But I realize there are a lot of things we need to discuss. I would rather spend just a little more time getting to know you before everything becomes even more complicated."

Meg's smile returned as she answered. "I think that's a fine idea, Your Highness, though I hope nothing ever becomes as *complicated* as this."

Varden held onto her hand as he leaned in closer. Meg closed her eyes and lifted her face. Suddenly, she jerked her head back.

"Jerald!" she exclaimed.

"Jerald?" Varden asked in confusion.

"Yes, Jerald!" Meg looked at Ty. "Ty, I completely forgot!"

Varden heard a loud <<croak>> and looked down. A large, ugly toad leaped towards them. It quickly disappeared. All of a sudden, Jerald appeared in its place.

"Jerald?! What are you doing here?" Varden asked, trying very hard not to laugh. "I assumed you would be cowering in your castle."

Jerald huffed and stood.

"That – that witch!" He pointed at Lara. "That witch turned me into a frog!"

"A toad," Lara corrected him.

"And then she sent these two hawks to come and kill me! They grabbed me and flew off with me and put me in their nest! They were going to eat me alive! I barely managed to escape! Varden, that witch tried to kill me! What are you going to do about it? I demand swift and fatal punishment!"

"Those are some substantial accusations," Varden spoke. "Do you have any proof?"

"Proof?" Jerald sputtered. "Proof?! You just saw it with your own eyes!"

"I'm sorry. I didn't see anything. Did you?"

"No, nothing," Meg answered.

Killian called over to him, "I saw you, but I didn't notice any difference."

"Don't tell me you're all afraid of that witch!" Jerald accused them. "Someone must have seen it!"

Varden took Meg's hand and walked away.

"No, Jerald," he spoke, "I doubt anyone did."

Chapter 27: If Bells Still Chime

The servants were already gone since Katie had given them the day off. So, she answered the door herself and let Ty, Killian, and Lara inside.

"Are you ready?" Killian asked her.

"In a moment, but I was wondering if I could actually speak to Ty first."

"Oh, of course," Ty answered. "Shall we go to the library?"

Katie nodded, and Ty followed her. After they walked in, she shut the door quietly and moved closer to him.

"I just," she stuttered, "Everything has been so busy lately, and I know after the wedding, things will only get busier, so I wanted to talk to you now while I have a chance."

"Okay." Ty nodded.

Katie nodded her head too. She clasped her hands together, smiled, looked away, looked back at Ty, looked up.

"Actually, aren't we going to be late?"

"Katie," Ty spoke. "I want to try again. With you."

"I want that too. I just wish you had given me a chance to say it," she said with a laugh.

"Of course. Next time."

Katie still looked hesitant.

"Is there something else?" Ty asked.

"Well . . . "She raised her hands then dropped them to her side. "I thought after I said that, you would try to kiss me or something."

"Oh," Ty said in surprise. "I didn't want to assume anything."

"Well," Katie shrugged, "now you don't have to assume."

Ty laughed quietly. He put his hand under her chin, bent his head, and kissed her. They both heard the door open but didn't pull away.

"Kate!" Lara yelled.

Katie stepped back and blushed.

"What are you doing? You said you wanted to take things slowly!" Lara scolded.

"I know. I did. I'm sorry. I just forgot."

"It's my fault," Ty spoke.

"I don't care who's fault it is. I – just go. Come on. We'll be late."

"I'm almost ready," Katie said as she dashed out of the room.

Ty followed her. Lara sighed and placed her hand over her face. Killian stepped in and reclined against the door frame.

"She said she would take it slowly!"

"Hmm," Killian answered.

"I can't believe this!"

"Well, you'd better believe it. "

Lara grunted. She reached into her pocket and slapped a coin on Killian's outstretched hand.

"I can't believe it," she said again.

"Now, Lara, no one likes a sore loser. I'll tell you what I'll do: I'll give you a chance to win it back."

"No."

"I'll bet you the same amount that at Varden's reception, Aidan and Alma will get up to dance before Ty and Kate."

"Aidan doesn't dance."

"So, it's a wager?"

"No!"

Killian smirked as Lara stormed out of the library. Everyone's mood was cheery by the time they reached the cathedral. They even arrived early. However, Lara did not stay for the entire ceremony. Before Varden and Meg finished saying their vows, the elderly bell-ringer found Lara and quietly asked her to join him outside.

"It's those terrible boys again," he explained. He led her to the bell tower. "You know King Varden wants me to ring these as soon as he's married, but I can't get to the ropes! Those terrible boys climbed up and put them up on a small ledge out of reach!"

"What do you want me to do?" Lara asked.

"Can't you create a wind to bring them down like last time?"

"No, my powers aren't strong yet."

"What about your brother? Where is he?"

"Mendel left a month ago."

"Then what am I to do?"

"Go get a ladder."

"But the priest stores the ladder at his home. By the time I get it, it will be too late. Don't you have any other suggestions?"

"No."

"Oh, dear, dear, dear."

The old man ran off. Lara stood and looked up at the ropes. She focused her eyes and raised her hand. A soft breeze moved them slightly. She tried again, but was unsuccessful. She wasn't strong enough yet. She lowered her hand. She would have to run after the bell-ringer and help him find the ladder.

A breeze came from behind her, swirling up to the ropes and shaking them loose. They dropped down. Lara turned around in surprise.

"How did you do that?"

Katie smiled and said, "I guess I forgot to tell you I've been practicing."

Lara smiled. She looked through the cathedral window.

"It looks like it's time."

"Shall we?" asked Katie.

"I believe we shall."

They both grabbed the ropes and began to pull. The bells rang throughout the kingdom, welcoming Callaway's new queen.

THE END

Author's Note

I first began planning this series with the intention of making an adaptation. The story I planned to adapt has several different versions. One is called *The Wild Swans* by Hans Christian Andersen, and another is *The Six Swans* recorded by the brothers Grimm. The stories are about a princess who has taken a vow of silence and must sew shirts of nettles in order to save her brothers. Her brothers have all been transformed into swans by an evil witch.

In my original plot, a poor girl and her brothers break into a witch's home and steal food. The brothers eat, but the girl is too scared to join them. The witch catches them and transforms the brothers into birds. The girl tells the witch they only stole the food because she had complained about being hungry, so the witch tells her she can break the spell if she remains silent for many years (I forget how many years I had planned). However, I kept revising the plot. Instead of multiple brothers turning into birds, there was one brother who became a pig. The girl didn't take any vow of silence but instead was usually quiet and reserved by choice due to her personality. I then decided to give her a friend with a contrasting personality, someone bubbly and chatty. This became Katie.

I called the main antagonist of Spellbound "the count"

because I was inspired by Thomas Borchert's portrayal of Count Dracula in the German musical fittingly titled: *Dracula: Das Musical*. I wanted to play with the idea of a young woman, Katie, being drawn to the antagonist similar to the way Mina is drawn to Dracula in the musical. I wanted Katie to feel a connection to the count and, due to her naivety, believe it to be something deeper than infatuation. However, my count became a lot creepier than I intended. I enjoy writing most of my antagonists, but the count is my least favorite character to date.

In *Charmed*, I wanted to expand on Varden's character a bit more. He was more rude and distrustful of Lara in the rough draft of my first book, but by the time I finished revising, he was actually friendly. The relationship between Varden and Lara grew in the second book to where he not only respected Lara, he trusted her. He also trusted Vivian which was unfortunate, but I wanted to show him in a vulnerable light. He was king, but that didn't mean he always knew what to do.

Aidan was also introduced in the second book, more as a random extra than a main character. However, in this third book, I found that his scenes were very enjoyable for me to write and seemingly just as entertaining for others to read. I'm glad his role got bigger.

I knew Mendel had to leave, but I couldn't help but bring him back in *Entranced*, even for a little bit. He couldn't stay for long though. He had to return to whatever he was doing. Perhaps one day I will discover what adventures he had and write about them.

This series took far longer to write than anticipated, but I'm pleased with it. Lara is one of my favorite characters of any of my books. In this series, she's definitely my favorite; though Jerald is a close second. I hope you enjoyed reading this as much as I enjoyed writing it.

Sincerely,

Rachel Peterson

(Jibber Jabber)

Preview: Luna Lore
Chapter 1

I would consider myself to be relatively normal.

I know I'm a little different. First of all, I am a princess, but that's not really a big deal, at least not for me. I have three older siblings, so they're closer in line to the throne than I am. Besides, girls don't inherit the kingdom. They do in some kingdoms, but not ours; so I don't have to worry about it.

I'm the only one in my family that has dark hair. All of my siblings and both of my parents have blonde hair. My mother's hair used to be dark, but it changed after she gave birth to Amelia, the oldest. It was a hard labor, and the stress turned her hair blonde. Amelia's hair used to be dark, and so was Aria's, my other sister. Mother said their hair changed color when they got older and that mine will change too. I hope she's right. I'm already ten, and it hasn't changed yet.

There's only one more thing that makes me different from everyone else: I have terrible nightmares. I don't know if I have them every night, but it feels like I do. I usually can't remember them. I know I'm running away. Something terrifying chases me. Whatever it is, it's always right behind me. I can't get away until I wake up.

"What is your opinion, Princess Noreen?"

Blast! I've been daydreaming again. Genevieve must have noticed. What was she going on about? History. Uprisings.

"Princess Noreen?"

"Yes," I answer. "I would say that the Ecklers dealt with the situation well. The Sindrell classes were clearly wrong to have started an unnecessary and unprovoked rebellion."

Always side with the Ecklers , at least if Genevieve is tutoring.

Genevieve nods her head and continues her lecture. I glance at my siblings. Amelia is the oldest at thirteen. She and my brother Declan look bored. I guess they've heard this lesson before. Aria seems to be paying attention, but that doesn't mean much. She always looks like she's paying attention even if she's not. She's only a year older, but she likes to act like I'm much younger than her. She tells me I'm odd and that she's more mature than I am.

Lastly, I glance at Owen. He seems to be trying to listen, but it's hard for him to concentrate. He's only five. I wish he didn't have to start being tutored yet. He doesn't seem ready. He's so little.

At last, Genevieve wraps everything up and dismisses us for the day, or what's left of the day. I don't like it when she keeps us stuck inside for so long. There might not be enough time left for me to even go outside. As soon as I start to leave, an attending maid approaches me to tell me I need to go to my bedroom. Guess I was right.

Mother is reclining in a chair when I get there. On the table near my bed, a drink waits for me. Mother always gives me something to drink each night to help with the nightmares. I don't think it works. They've only become worse.

"Help her change into her nightclothes," Mother directs the maid.

"It's still light out. I don't have to go to bed yet."

"It will be nighttime soon, Princess Noreen," the servant counters. "It's best to get ready now so you can get a good rest."

The maids know who to side with. They must agree with the king, then the queen. I'm much lower on the chain of command.

I change my clothes and crawl into bed. I don't feel like brushing my hair, and Mother doesn't press the matter. The maid leaves, and Mother strolls over to me.

"It's not fair," I complain. "It's not even dark out yet. I hate being stuck inside."

"At least you have these." Mother points to the potted plants scattered throughout the room. "It's as though the outdoors has been brought to you."

"It's not the same thing."

"Here, drink your medicine."

She hands me the cup, but I turn my head and try to wave it off.

"I don't like it. I don't want to drink it tonight."

"It will help you sleep."

"I don't want to sleep. I don't want to have nightmares."

"Drink your medicine, Noreen."

I'm frustrated, but I don't have a choice. I take the cup and start sipping it. I'll drink it, but I'll do it at my own pace. I get halfway through when my bedroom door opens. Owen steps inside.

"I want to play with Nona," he pleads.

That's his name for me. I love that name, and I love being an older sister. Even before he was born, I was excited to not be the youngest anymore. I remember playing with him once when he was a baby. Mother was whispering to Father. She didn't think I could hear. She said, "If only he had been a girl." Father answered, "Next time." This made me sad to think that they were disappointed in Owen, so I tried to love him even more.

"Owen, you need to go to bed too," orders Mother.

She strides to the door and calls out for a maid to take him to his room. I glare down at the medicine. I'm tired of drinking it. I look back at Mother then quickly pour the rest of the drink into the plant near my bed. Mother returns, takes the empty cup, and bids me goodnight.

I hope that I will be able to stay awake. I can't dream if I'm awake. I think I still drank too much of the medicine. If I lay my head down, I would be more comfortable. I don't have to close my eyes. I don't want to accidentally fall asleep. I lay quietly for a few minutes. I decide to close my eyes anyway. I'll stay awake, but I'll rest my eyes for just a little bit. I'm getting drowsier. I think I am falling asleep.

As my eyes are closed, I feel as though I'm being lifted. I seem to be flying through the air. I don't open my eyes because I like this dream. The floating stops, and I'm lying down again. I look up, but I don't see my bedroom. There are trees everywhere. I must be in the forest. Obviously, I'm not in the forest since this is just a dream. I reach down and touch the grass. It's soft and cold. This dream is different from my other ones. Everything seems more real. I walk towards one of the trees. It's hard to keep my eyes open. I'm still so tired, and everything looks blurry. I'll just lie down again and hope to wake up back in my room.

It's dark when I open my eyes. I'm still in the forest, and my vision is hazy. That's how it is in dreams. I never can see clearly. As I get up, I step on something sharp. I start to look down but then give up. I'm too tired to care.

I take a few steps then stop. Something is watching me. The frightening thing from my dreams must be here. I turn around and hear it moving through the bushes. I don't think I should run. I'll try to sneak away. I move quietly but quickly away from the bushes. I tip-toe towards what looks like a small cliff.

I step closer to the edge then freeze. I can hear it. It wasn't behind me. It's in the ditch below the cliff. I can hear it breathing. I step back. My heart is beating so quickly. I don't want it to see me. I don't even want to know what it is. Is that wrong? Shouldn't I be facing my fears? I don't want to be a coward.

I tentatively step forward and lean over the edge. Glowing yellow eyes peer up at me. It's a huge dark beast. It opens his mouth, and I see its razor sharp teeth and fangs. It stares angrily at me and makes a dreadful noise. It's not a roar. It sounds like a shrill scream.

I run away from the cliff, but the beast follows me. I'm too scared to look back. I have to keep running. I can hear it breathing right behind me. I don't want to die. I don't want it to hurt me.

Wait. It can't hurt me. It's just a dream. There's no reason to be scared. I take a chance and turn around. I don't see the beast anymore. I still hear it. It must be nearby, but it's no longer chasing me.

I must have closed my eyes again, because when I open them, I'm back in my room. It's morning. My bedroom is the same. There is no forest, no beast, nothing to fear. I pull off the blanket and hop out of bed.

"Ow!" I exclaim.

I lift up my left leg and sit back down. A long thorn protrudes from the bottom of my foot. I touch it. It hurts too much to pull it out. One of the maids knocks and enters my room. I show her the thorn.

"You must have stepped on one of your plants," she says.

I nod. I must have. Why don't I believe it?

She removes the thorn for me. She calls it a splinter though. I don't appreciate her down-playing my pain, but I know she's only trying to help.

I see through my window that it's dark and cloudy outside. I start scratching my arms. On overcast days, my arms and legs itch since my hair gets thicker. I don't feel well on cloudy days. Mother usually makes me stay in my room. Sure enough, before I'm even finished getting dressed, Mother enters and tells the maid that I have to stay in bed today.

I wish I could go outside, but I need to obey. I go back into bed and resign myself to a boring day. I try to read but can't concentrate. I keep thinking about my dream. I want to draw the beast. I can't remember what it looked like. I didn't get a clear view.

I wait all day for Owen. I know he'll come see me once tutoring is over. I also know he'll help me if I ask him.

"Nona!"

At last, he's here. He runs to the bed and hugs me. He brought some papers with him.

"Do you want to read the story?" I ask.

"Yes, and I can help read it."

He jumps on the bed and sits in my lap. He hands me the papers that contain the story. It's not a book like the ones Genevieve makes us read. It's a story I wrote for him about snakes. I know Owen likes reading about snakes.

"I need your help with something."

"Reading?" he asks.

"No, when Mother comes in to give me my medicine, I want you to come back and ask her to take you to your room."

"The maids always take me to my room."

"I know, but I want you to ask her. Do you think you can do that for me?"

He nods.

"I can do that."

"Ok. Don't forget."

I start reading the story to him. I stop at the smaller words so he can read them. He's getting better at recognizing the letters and sounding out the words. He can read many of them, but he gets tired and needs a break sometimes.

Lucy, one of the attending maids, enters to help me get ready for bed. I whisper to Owen, reminding him to come back, and he leaves me with Lucy. I like Lucy. She's gentle when she brushes my hair. She says she likes my dark hair color even though I don't.

When she's finished, Mother enters and dismisses Lucy. I crawl into bed. Mother walks over with the cup of medicine. I reach out my hand to take it as Owen opens the door and steps inside.

"Go to bed, Owen," Mother softly orders.

She still has the cup. Owen came to the room too early. Mother was supposed to hand me the cup first. I need Owen as a distraction so I can dump the medicine. I have to see if my dream was really a dream.

"Could you take me to my room, Mother?" he dutifully asks.

"One of the maids will take you. Lucy!" Mother calls out.

Mother walks to the door. I jump out of bed.

"I can take him, Mother," I offer.

I need a chance to ask Owen to come back again.

"No, you stay in bed. Here, take this." She hands me the cup. "Lucy will take him."

She ushers Owen to the door as Lucy enters the room. Mother instructs her to take Owen away. She's turned away from me. I quickly dump the medicine out the window and return to bed. With Mother watching, I pretend to drink the liquid. I do it several times because it usually takes a few swallows to drink all of it. I hand her cup. I pretend to go to sleep, and she leaves the room. I close my eyes, but I don't feel tired. I lay there waiting. It would be nice if I don't fall asleep tonight, but I'm afraid of seeing the beast whether or not I sleep.

I hear someone entering my room. Owen? I carefully peek. It's not my brother. It's my father. He picks me up and carries me to the corner of the room. I keep my eyes closed until he stops. He moves one of the large plants and reaches up to touch a crevice in the wall. He pushes it, and part of the wall moves over to the left. I have a secret passageway in my room! He turns to look at me. I close my eyes again. He takes me behind the wall and carries me down many steps. When we reach the bottom, I see we're in an enormous underground tunnel.

A horse is tethered waiting for us. Father lifts me up and sits behind me. The horse trots forward. I wonder if I should tell him I'm awake. If we're going on an adventure, I should be awake to help. I decide to pretend to sleep for a little longer.

At the end of the tunnel, there's another door. We get off the horse, and Father carries me through the entry. Now we're outside – in a forest. I close my eyes again as he sets me on the ground. I hear him walk away and close the door.

I sit up. I don't see the door. There's only a large hill. Wait. If I look closely, I can barely make out the outline of a door. Why is Father acting so secretive? I look around me. This forest looks like the forest in my dream. I wasn't dreaming at all. It *was* real.

I shift my hand behind me to get up. It touches something, something with fur. Dread overtakes me. I slowly turn my head to look up at the beast standing behind me, but the beast isn't there. I look down. I hadn't touched the beast. A small dead goat is lying beside me. Father must have put it there, but I don't know why.

I hear a noise in the bushes and stand up. A bird flies out of them. It was only a bird. The trees start to sway, but it's only the wind. This doesn't reassure me. I don't think I'm alone. If the forest was real, the beast must be real too. At least now I know how I can escape.

I run to the hidden door. I push against it, but it doesn't open. I must have to pull on it. I pull at the handle. I push again. It's not moving. I start banging my fists against it.

"Let me in! Father! Father! Let me in!"

I keep pulling and pushing and banging against the door. I start crying. I'm scared. It's getting dark. I can't be out here. I hear another noise. Was that the wind? I don't know, but the beast is coming. It will probably eat the goat and then eat me. Is that what Father wanted? Is the goat here to lure the beast to me?

"Father! Don't let it eat me! Please! Let me in! I'm scared!"

My hands are sore from banging and prying at the handle. I'm terrified and feel light-headed. My face is wet from tears. I have to keep trying.

I hear a growl, and lose hope. I shut my eyes and lean against the door, exhausted. There's nothing I can do. I'm going to die. I'm going to die.

I open my eyes, and it's completely dark. I must have fallen asleep. I'm leaning against one of the trees. Was I carried there? I see the door up ahead and walk towards it. There's no wind. The air is completely still. I stare down at the goat, what's left of the goat. Now that I think of it, I might have heard the beast eating. It had seemed so close to me, but I had been too scared to open my eyes. The beast must have eaten the goat, but it didn't eat me.

I hear its breathing. I know it can see me. What if I misjudged the beast? Just because something is scary, that doesn't make it evil. Maybe it doesn't want to hurt me. I look for its yellow eyes, but I can't find them. I start to walk to see if it will follow me. I hear another sound up ahead. A bird? I'm not sure. I remember the cliff. Maybe the beast is there again.

I move slowly. I don't want to startle it. Now that I'm not under the influence of the medicine, I can see much clearer. The small cliff is more of an overhanging rock. I reach the rock and look over. My guess was correct. The beast was hiding below.

It stares up at me. It reminds me of a very large leopard. I've seen drawings of them in books, but the beast doesn't have the leopard's spots. Its fur is short and a dark grey. I move to the side, and it follows me. It has black stripes on its back and face, but no spots. Its yellow eyes watch me, but they don't seem as scary now.

I reach down to see if it will let me pet it. It moves its paw towards me. I back away startled. The beast shows its teeth but, surprisingly, backs away as well. Perhaps he is as scared of me as I am of him. I watch his face as I reach out to touch its paw. It seems to trust me. It moves the front paw towards me. It feels wet like blood. Has the beast been injured? I chance to look down.

That's when I notice the water ripples. I look back up in shock. I've been staring at my own reflection.

You can find the rest of this story for free at

https://jibberjabberblog.blogspot.com/p/blog-page.html

or for purchase at Amazon.com.

ABOUT THE AUTHOR

You can find Jibber Jabber (Rachel Peterson) on twitter @JJabbertweets or at https://jibberjabberblog.blogspot.com/

www.ingramcontent.com/pod-product-compliance
Lightning Source LLC
Chambersburg PA
CBHW050940120626
46552CB00001B/299